TRAP HOUSE

WITH[...]N

Sa'id Salaam

STREET CHRONICLES

TRAP HOUSE:

Cover Design: Hot Book Covers
                  www.hotbookcovers.com

Typesetting: G&S Typesetting & Ebook Conversions
                  info@gstypesetting.com

ISBN: 978-0-9834311-6-9
LCCN: 2011938348

Join us on Facebook, G Street Chronicles Fan Page
Follow us on Twitter, @gstrtchroni

Acknowledgements

First and foremost, All Praise is for Allah! The most gracious, who taught the Qur'an, created man and taught him eloquent speech.

Next, to the woman who gave me life and class...my mother, Diedra, and then the woman who did the same for her...Grandma Rainey.

To my Ummah worldwide, may the peace, blessing and mercy of Allah be upon us all.

To Amira, Zakiyyah, Halima, Abdul-Haseeb, Khalif, Khalil and Iyana...we will always be family.

My children Erv-G, Derrick and whats her face.

To those of my family who supported me, I can not thank you enough. I have a lot of words in me, but none adequately express what you mean to me.

To all my dudes trapped in the belly...keep ya heads up. Specifically: Stack (Cascade) Slim, Zaki, Zaid, Kabir, All the Abdullah's, Sayyid (Sav) Omari, Makeen, Ali Rock, Boon, Signature (Bx), Knowledge, Subur, KG (Albany), Abdur-rasheed (Columbus), Paul (Snoop) Mobley, John Sabir, Hamza (Sweet!), Skeem Aleem, Ketchup, Ali (Brick City), Talib, Sideeq, As-sideeq, Basir, Isa, both Qawi's, Amir(Young Money) Rafi, Donald, Sharif, 1440, Hakim, Yi, Andrew Mayes, K.O. (Bx) Buckhead, Milk, B-bop, Dex, Bilal and anyone I forgot.

Also Tariq Khan (Quran and Sunnah), Imam Shamsid-Deen,

Bunny, Kimani Chris Barnes (Bx), Lisa Jones (Bx). My ATL people, Terry B-large, Fernando, Dwayne, Tack, Ant, Derrick (Rap City) Tucker, Dondi Gant, Omen (Bx), O-P, King Stan, and the whole city of Atlanta, my second home!

My dude Sherm…good looking out, putting me on the team. Let's take it to the next level!

And finally, all of my brand new fans. Thank you. I appreciate the support. God willing…this is just the beginning.

Holla Back
Said.salaam@gmail.com

Dedicated to:

Zakiyyah Nix-Salaam
Laylah (ride or die)

Trap House n.) A place in which drugs are bought, sold and or consumed.

Crack (krak) n.) (slang) A highly potent and purified form of cocaine for smoking.

Junkie (Jun' ke) n.) 1. A narcotics addict 2. One who is addicted to a specified activitiy.

FOREWARD

The demographics of Atlanta were changing as rapidly as the city's skyline. Not only were new condos and high-rise apartment buildings sprouting up daily, but more ambitious projects were on the horizon.

Miniature cities, like Atlantic Station and the beltline, were being built within the borders of the city. Entire neighborhoods, like East Atlanta, Kirkwood, and Vine City were transforming overnight.

The rapid gentrification caused real estate prices to soar. Poorer residents who could no longer afford to live in the neighborhoods where they were born and raised were forced out to the surrounding suburbs, where the cost of living was slightly easier to tolerate.

The irony of all of it was, those suburbs were once home to all whites, but when the blacks moved in, it drove the property values in their enclave down. The resulting "white flight" left instant ghettos in its wake.

As in most impoverished areas of our great country where hope and opportunity are in short supply, the demand for illegal drugs was heightened. Atlanta became one of the few cities left in America where open drugs markets still flourished. Places like "the Bluff," Peachtree, and Pine, and "the Horseshoe," operated full blast like drug bazaars, providing one-stop shopping for the morally challenged. They sold anything and everything, from crack to blunts to blow jobs. For decades, they operated with seeming impunity.

As the population shifted from black to white, the transition was tumultuous at best. The incoming whites were viewed as easy prey, and they were quickly preyed upon. Any white person caught in one of these transitional neighborhoods ran the risk of being robbed…or worse. The kids who attended nearby colleges were bait. Carjackings, armed robberies, and kidnappings were daily occurrences.

Many a housing rehab or new project was forced to start from scratch because the local junkies would steal all the materials without a second thought. These thefts did not only include two-by-fours or sheet rock left unsecured by naïve contractors, but absolutely anything of value. Newly installed plumbing was stripped out overnight. Bricks, bags of cement, and anything that could be resold would be stolen.

Anyone who was foolish enough to forget to lock their car may as well have just given it away, because as sure as the sun rises, it would be gone by dawn. Tennis rackets, baby seats, and anything left inside an unlocked car were also fair game.

Not only were crimes like vandalism and theft on the rise, but Atlanta was a just plain dangerous place to be. The robbery and murder of boxer Vernon Foster made national headlines, but in actuality, that was only one of six similar incidents that occurred that very same night.

Crime in the city rose at an alarming rate as droves of feral youth roamed the city, victimizing anyone they found who was brave or stupid enough to be out after dark.

* * *

The skyrocketing crime rate proved to be a major issue in the election of the city's new mayor. The outgoing mayor, who had done an excellent job boosting the city's profile, was soft on crime. She slashed the police department's budget to the point where they became virtually useless within the community that so desperate needed their help. While she did order the upgrade of the dilapidated water and sewage systems and the building of new sidewalks, if anyone was caught on one of those new sidewalks after dark, the chances of being raped, robbed, or killed were still high.

Although there were three qualified candidates in the race for mayor, only two were seriously considered. The first of the likely candidates was the current sheriff, who ran, of course, on the law and order platform. He ran graphic campaign ads showing footage from actual crime scenes, driving home the fact that Atlanta was a dangerous place and claiming that he was the man to clean it up.

The other serious contender for the mayoral position was a city councilman who touted his twenty years in politics and his close relationship with the incumbent among his qualifications. He was well liked and able to share credit for the accomplishments that had been made in the city during her term of office. However, as the campaign wore on, it seemed a new skeleton fell out of the second candidate's closet each and every day. Racy e-mails traced to his personal Blackberry exposed his penchant for young girls and, as he called it, "dookie love." By the end of the campaign, he looked like the bone collector.

The almost-forgotten underdog was a thirty-seven-year-old investment banker who had zero political experience. As the only white candidate in a predominantly black city, he was not taken very seriously—at first. Tom Haskin did have a grassroots campaign that was becoming a movement—Obama in reverse, if you will—especially as younger black voters came into the fold. His unique, ambitious ideas on deterring crime seemed to make sense and attracted attention, as all else had failed up to that point. Using his acumen in the financial world, he had plans to balance the city's dismal budget as well.

While the two front runners engaged in smear tactics and dirty tricks, Tom stuck to the issues. Debates turned into ugly two-way arguments that made the councilman and the sheriff appear petty, while Haskins was basically ignored. When asked a question, he gave brief, precise, honest answers devoid of the rhetoric his opponents seemed to rely upon.

Tom Haskins also wisely wooed the Latino population of the city that the front runners seemed to forget about or ignore. Come election day, the sheriff and the councilman split 80 percent of the black vote, and the rest of the ballots were cast in Haskins favor. The remaining 20 percent, along with all of the white and Latino vote was enough to push Haskins over the top. And just like that, the underdog banker became the city's first white mayor in decades.

* * *

As promised, the first order of business was the failing budget. Haskins viewed it as a failing company and took the necessary steps to save it. First, he renegotiated its debt, freeing up a ton of cash. And then he took a look at the tax system.

Ordinarily, raising taxes would be a death sentence for any official, but 90 percent of Atlantans were in favor of a one-year increase to directly support the police and fire services.

Being the product of hippie parents, Tom had a soft spot for users, but he had no love for dealers. Recent statistics indicated that drugs were the underlying factor of 80 percent of the crime occurring in the city. He planned to combat the drug problem aggressively by pushing the pushers into prisons and the addicts into rehabs.

With the help of the county judges and the sheriff, he was able to implement an extensive rehabilitation program to help users get clean and stay clean. Users of anything harder than marijuana involved in a crime were sent to a two-year lockdown program, followed by intensive probation and after-care. Haskins and the officials pushed for and passed new legislation that would send dealers away for a long time. Parole was abolished for drug crimes committed within the city of Atlanta.

It took a few months for the streets to get the message. Since county judges refused to set bond for drug dealers, who would just use drug money to pay them, the word spread quickly.

Police targeted the legions of zombie junkies who care-lessly roamed the city streets. Once caught, the addicts would gladly trade their freedom for information on their dealers. Not only were they given a free pass when caught with drugs, but they were allowed to keep them as a bounty for snitching. It was an offer few of them could refuse.

Thus, dealers were not only forced from behind closed doors, but they also had to be extremely selective as to who they sold to. They began to set up smokehouses for their customers. The days were cop-and-go were over. "If you smoke, sit down and smoke," they had to explain. "No drugs leave the premises."

The smokehouses, commonly known as traphouses, varied by the diverse class and spending habits of their clientele. Some were plush, boasting full bars, wide-screen TVs, catered food, and waitresses. Others were as rundown as the street dwellers who frequented them. This climate gave rise to an upcoming hustler with disgusting sexual fetishes and a sick sense of humor.

But since P.I.G. had the best blow in town, he was the man.

CHAPTER 1

P.I.G. stood six-four (when he stood) and tipped the scales at a hair shy of 600 pounds. His light complexion, "high yella," as it was called, complemented his sandy brown hair that was always braided in intricate designs. He wasn't one of those big handsome fat dudes. P.I.G. was disgusting. He had a large, bulbous nose covered with blackheads and a nasty-looking keloid the size of a softball behind his ear. His eyes were far too small for his huge face, giving him an amphibious look. Even if P.I.G. were to lose 300 or 400 pounds, he would still be an ugly monster of a man.

In school, he was teased unmercifully, almost to the point of torture. Not only his size, but also his odor was a subject of ridicule. Being a large child, it was difficult for him to adequately clean himself at times, resulting in a sickening body aroma that was a mixture of sweat, urine, and feces. Even some of the more immature teachers openly teased him.

He was a huge fan of the late rapper, The Notorious B.I.G., and often recited his lyrics. In fact, at one point, the majority of his conversations were excerpts from those songs. As a result, he earned the name The Notorious P.I.G. It was meant as a dis, but he didn't mind it in the least. P.I.G. knew he was fat, and being mentioned in the likes of his hero didn't bother him one bit.

P.I.G.'s childhood was pure hell. If not for his next-door neighbor and only friend, it would have been far worse. Earl was a bit of an outcast himself due to his heavy Caribbean accent and off-brand clothing. Like most immigrants to this country, Earl's parents were hard workers and frugal, not accustomed to wasting money. So, they denied their son of some of the extras that were the norm for most kids, like name brand clothing, for one. They couldn't understand why American parents spent hundreds on a pair of sneakers or jeans when Walmart was right down the street.

Meanwhile, P.I.G.'s parents lavished him with everything his heart desired. Perhaps it was recompense for their poor parenting skills or for allowing their child to overeat himself into oblivion. He had every game, toy, and gadget at his disposal, and the pantry stayed stocked with every food P.I.G. desired.

Being his only friend, Earl was a collateral beneficiary of P.I.G.'s parents' generosity. P.I.G. shared everything with him, using that as a means to be the leader among them.

Once he matured a bit, he realized that some people played up to him to reap some of the benefits of being his friend. He knew they were using him, so he used them back and made them pay with their dignity—anything from having kids walk miles to Mickey D's in the scorching heat, to having them consume odd things for money. A raw onion could earn a kid a dollar, while a bottle of Tabasco sauce might warrant a five. Kids tried to use P.I.G., so he used them for his own entertainment. He soon learned that money meant power, and power was the shit!

Occasionally, someone got bold enough to try to take something from P.I.G., but that meant dealing with Earl, and since taking from P.I.G. took from Earl, nobody dared take a thing from P.I.G..period.

CHAPTER 2

P.I.G. owned and operated traphouses of every level all over the city. Some catered to professionals who liked to smoke their crack in comfort, while others were absolute dumps in the heart of the ghetto.

His headquarters consisted of a modest one-story brick house on Moreland Avenue. It had once contained three bedrooms, two baths, and a kitchen unit, but P.I.G. remodeled it. He closed off the kitchen, incorporating it with the master bedroom. It was where P.I.G. cooked and cut and processed the dope, and he also used it as his living space.

The rest of the rooms were gutted out into one large area adjoined to the living room. This room was for the smokers. The walls were lined with sofas and large pillows for customers to lounge on. In the middle of the room was a large open area dubbed "the stage."

Although his other houses did the majority of his business, P.I.G. preferred to be there where the action was. These were the customers who spent thousands and the ones most likely to entertain. They were the freaks who would do anything if enough crack was involved.

After petty arguments among the junkies turned violent a few times, P.I.G. started Friday night fights. The affair was complete with weigh-ins and all the pre-fight hype of authentic matchups.

Most of the time there were sex acts of varying vulgarity going on around the room. P.I.G. kept a state-of-the-art digital camcorder hooked to a large plasma screen mounted on the wall. This way, he could watch all the perversions and save them for posterity.

* * *

P.I.G. glanced around at the occupants of the room with disdain. Everyone was feverishly pulling on their straight-shooters, oblivious to his need to be entertained. His curiosity was suddenly piqued by an escalating exchange of words between two junkies.

"Bitch! Didn't I tell yo' funky ass not to push my stem," yelled Mojo, one of the regulars. He was upset that Kim, another fixture, and pushed his pipe in his absence.

Crack pipes, known as "shooters" or "stems," will accumulate a great deal of residue that can be pushed to either end and smoked again. Most junkies use this once their supply runs out, but when Mojo made a beer run, Kim cleaned out his stem.

"Shit, nigga! You took too long," Kim shot back.

"Bitch, it don' matter how long I took. That's my shit!" Mojo replied, now standing over her.

Kim knew the next words out of her mouth meant the difference between getting the shit slapped out of her and possibly getting some more to smoke, so she chose her words carefully. "Aww, chill out, baby," she purred, rubbing her palm against his crotch. "I'll make it up to you."

P.I.G. saw a freak show on the horizon and decided to help it along. "Go on and give him some of that dome. I'll set something out once y'all done."

"Man, that don't do shit for them grams she pushed out ma shit," Mojo complained meekly as he undressed. He was a hardcore junkie and couldn't care less about a blow job—or anything else, for that matter. He'd long smoked away his job, his wife, his kids, and his home. He preferred to smoke, but he knew a good performance to entertain P.I.G.'s whims would garner more than the reside Kim stole from him. Mojo dropped his pants, allowing his twelve-inch penis to swing free between his thighs like a clock pendulum, the claim to fame that allowed him entry to P.I.G.'s inner sanctum.

People who knew of P.I.G.'s licentious fetishes would bring freaks from far and wide. P.I.G. was known to pay a finder's fee for extraordinary sexual deviants.

Kim, likewise, was kept around for her ability to swallow objects like twelve-inch penises. If not for crack, she could have had a career as a sword swallower or a circus freak. She was said to give the best head in the world. Given the fact that she could not only get a crackhead up but off, the rumor was probably true.

P.I.G. trained his camera on the couple, filling the fifty-five-inch screen with the action. To everyone's relief, Mojo got an erection; given the amount of cocaine he'd consumed, that was no small feat. He was "ooh"-ing and "ahh"-ing for P.I.G.'s benefit as he long-stroked Kim's face. She maintained eye contact with P.I.G., gagging loudly every time Mojo pushed past her larynx.

P.I.G. began rocking back and forth as if he was the one

deep down in Kim's throat. He had a raging hard-on, but masturbating was out of the question. It was not that he was above it, but he was simply too fat to get a good grip on himself.

The couple knew that P.I.G. could get excited enough to ejaculate from visual stimulation alone, and they could tell by the looks of him that he was close. Experience also taught them that prolonging the experience was to their benefit.

Kim pulled Mojo from her trachea and turned around. Mojo entered her from the back, pushing himself halfway up her spinal column. He was pounding away, putting on a great show, until the door of the bedroom opened, dashing their hopes of milking more dope out of P.I.G.

Blast emerged from the back room and surveyed the situation. She quickly ascertained what was going on and sprang into action. Without saying a word, she made her way over to P.I.G. and knelt in front of him. She removed him from his pants and took him in her mouth. A few strokes of her hand was all it took for P.I.G. to reach a slobbering, air-gasping orgasm. The show was over.

"Earl, set them out an eight ball," P.I.G. ordered once he regained his composure. He was up to a half-ounce in his mind until Blast came to the rescue.

CHAPTER 3

Blast wasn't just P.I.G.'s girl, but she also served as his right-hand man and was, in actuality, running the business. P.I.G. was merely a trick; it was because of her that he was successful.

Although Blast was a shade darker than tar and was completely flat-chested, it was obvious she was once very pretty. She was tall, rail thin with the seductive gait of a runway model. Her teeth had yellowed and were held in place by gray gums, a result of the drug use, but her smile could still melt ice. She rarely smiled much anymore, though, as life hadn't given her much to smile about.

Blast grew up in a rundown trailer along the Mississippi delta with her mother and eight siblings. The trailer was one of the many on Mr. Johnson's vast farm; he rented the trailers out to the help. In exchange for rent and a meager salary, the families all worked the farms in one capacity or another. Blast's two older brothers, along with a few older boys, did the heavy labor, while the children picked the fields. All of the mothers supplemented their incomes by trading sexual favors to Mr. Johnson for extras. As a direct result, most of the younger children on the farm were the product of that arrangement.

There were no men on the farm because once they were of age, they left their mothers, sisters, and younger brothers behind to be slaves to Mr. Johnson, mentally, physically, and sexually.

And that was exactly how Mr. Johnson viewed his workers: as slaves. He knew the younger ones were his offspring, but that didn't matter to him. He made everyone call him "Mister," and he trained his ears to hear "Master" whenever they said it.

Mr. Johnson would ride around the farm on his tractor pretending to be an overseer. "Get back to work, gal!" he'd bark at one. "Cotton's not gonna pick itself!" he'd gripe to another.

It was during one of these forays into his modern-day plantation that he noticed young Blast had ripened. At fourteen, she hadn't grown breasts to speak of, but the amount of butt cleavage peeking out from under her small shorts said she was ready. He had become so accustomed to the overweight mothers that the sight of Blast was too much for him to ignore. "Hey, gal!" he croaked through the sudden lump in his throat.

"Yassir, Mista? Blast replied meekly, lowering her gaze as she had been taught.

"Uh, I…well…um…" Mr. Johnson stammered, unsure how to proceed.

Blast heard the yearning in his voice and knew she was now in control. She knew giving up the pussy kept the older women out of the fields, and she had a pussy too. Like most of the kids on the plantation, she'd spied on her mother either fucking or sucking good ol' Mista. She'd also seen the exchange after the deed was done.

Blast looked Mr. Johnson dead in his eyes as she made her way over to where he was seated on the tractor. "I ain't hardly 'bout to suck yo' thang in this hot sun," she said, climbing aboard.

"Well, I guess we best go on to the house," Mister said eagerly as he put the tractor in gear.

Back at the house, Mr. Johnson explored young Blast's budding sexuality for the rest of the day, in two-minute increments. At the end of the day, Blast pocketed a couple of bucks for it and was out of the fields for good. Word spread quickly about the arrangement once the jilted mothers began to feel the pinch in their pocketbooks. When the older boys caught wind of how good Blast was in the sack, they all wanted a piece. Since they didn't have money like Mista to pay for it, they just took it. Anytime one of them caught Blast anywhere alone, they forced themselves on her and into her.

Once her brothers got in on the act, Blast decided it was time to go. She reasoned that if she was going to be treated like a whore, she should at least be paid like one. The day after her fifteenth birthday, she sucked Master to sleep and then cleaned out his money box. By the time the inhabitants of the farm realized she was gone, she was halfway to Atlanta.

Blast hadn't set both feet on the ground when Smooth spotted her. He was a chicken hawk who routinely stalked the bus stations in search of runaways. He liked them young, and with Blast's lack of breasts, he knew he could pass her off as thirteen. It only took Smooth ten seconds to recognize that she was alone. That wide-eyed gaze around the big city spoke volumes. There was no grandmother there go get her; she was completely on her own. Smooth had to move quick since he wasn't the only chicken hawk in town. He checked around once more to make sure no one was coming for her, and then he made his move.

Once he got her to his house, he fed her a steady diet of dick, game, and crack cocaine. Before she knew what hit her, she was standing on a corner, turning tricks with a nasty crack habit to support.

He pimped her so hard she had to sleep on her feet. If she begged for a rest, he put the rest of his foot up her ass and put her back to work.

One day, Smooth caught her sleeping on a park bench and wasted no time kicking her ass. P.I.G., who happened to be on the next bench getting a blow job from another crack whore, watched in anger. He frequented the park daily to relieve his sexual frustrations. He had recently discovered that paying in crack was not only cost effective, but also that crack whores always worked harder when there were drugs on the line. Although he was a coward, P.I.G. couldn't stand the sight of the young girl being beaten.

Before Smooth knew it, P.I.G. had him in the air, held by his throat. Smooth was hard on a bitch, but he was a bitch himself when confronted. P.I.G. tossed him in the grass once he passed out from the pressure on his windpipe. "Are you okay?" P.I.G. asked the battered girl.

"Do I look okay?" Blast replied, spitting blood.

"No, you don't," he answered, helping her to her feet. "Where do you want me to take you?" P.I.G. asked anxiously as Smooth began to stir.

"Take me with you," Blast said. She was as eager to leave before Smooth came to as P.I.G. was. She went with P.I.G. that day and had been with him ever since, fifteen years and counting.

Since she was no longer turning tricks and he was no longer buying them, Blast convinced P.I.G. to sell to support both of their habits. It turned out to be a win-win situation. Blast could smoke as much as she wanted, and P.I.G. practically lived in her mouth. He gave her the nickname of "Blast" because of the huge hits she could smoke. Likewise, she privately called him by his given name.

* * *

When Blast emerged from the back room, the freak show was canceled. She knew P.I.G. was still a trick at heart and would set out good dope to see the junkies perform. She intervened by giving him a quick blow job to release some steam.

As soon as Mojo saw her coming down the hall, he lost his huge erection. He pulled himself out of Kim's intestines and began to dress. The couple then smoked their pay in silence.

"If anybody else wanna put on a show, y'all can sweep up," P.I.G. chuckled as Blast cleaned the semen and saliva from him.

Those familiar with the term joined in the laughter. The ones who weren't laughed anyway just because P.I.G. laughed. Only one person wasn't the least bit amused. Wanda, a dancer, had stopped by to smoke a cocaine-laced blunt, and she openly scorned P.I.G. He was a friend of her boyfriend's, but she loathed the man. "You need to sweep up yo' damn self, ya nasty bastard," she spat venomously.

"Bitch, you'll be sweeping up sooner or later," P.I.G. shot back between chuckles. The feeling was mutual. P.I.G. hated Wanda. If it wasn't for all the money Mike put in his pocket on her behalf, he wouldn't have dealt with her at all. And if he didn't have the best dope in town, she wouldn't have stepped foot in his place.

"You first, muthafucker," Wanda said, taking a sizzling pull on the blunt.

"After you, ya spiteful bitch," P.I.G. retorted.

Mike did a lot of business with P.I.G., but P.I.G. longed for the day when Wanda came begging. He knew it would come one day, as it came for all junkies eventually. *Yeah, she's cool now with the fly mouth and all,* P.I.G. thought to himself, *but you can't smoke pure cocaine every day like she's doing and not fall off.* He knew the shit was inevitable, and when she did fall, P.I.G. would be right there, broom in hand.

CHAPTER 4

"Here we go again," Tiffany said inwardly as Marcus turned onto Moreland Avenue. She knew he was headed to see "the pig," as she called him.

A skinny crack whore darted in front of them, flagging down cars.

Tiffany sucked her pretty white teeth loudly when Marcus pulled to a stop in front of P.I.G.'s house.

"Don't start," he warned, dropping his high-pitched voice down a few octaves for effect.

"Start what?" Tiffany whined. "We come here every day now."

"Just give me the money, boo," he said sweetly, flashing that dazzling smile.

It did the trick, and Tiffany dug into her purse to pay for her boyfriend's drugs.

Marcus was short in stature and long in good looks. His chestnut-colored skin was offset by hazel eyes with flecks of gold in them. He had "good hair" that was wavy when short and curly when long. Although he only stood five-five, he made his clothes look damn good.

Tiffany was short as well, standing just under five feet. She possessed the smoothest black skin, and it seemed to glow. Her dark eyes were slightly slanted, giving her an exotic look. God had also given her a beautiful set of full lips that she kept highly shined with Mac lip gloss. She hated them, but most men got a semi just looking at them. Her headful of thick, healthy hair extended past her shoulders, but that didn't prevent her from gluing weaves in anyway. Like most dark-skinned women, she was conditioned to believe that beauty required a light complexion, green eyes, and straight hair. Since she possessed none of those traits, her self-esteem would not allow her to appreciate just how lovely she really was. That was a big part of why she was hanging on to Marcus for dear life. They had been together since seventh grade, no matter what shit he dragged her through.

"Boo, this is my last fifty bucks. It's got to last me until I get paid," Tiffany whined as she hand over her hard-earned money.

"I told you Ima give it back later. I got some money coming," Marcus replied, snatching the cash from her hands.

Tiffany mused to herself, *He always has money coming in "later." Only problem is, that "later" never comes.* She realized that besides filling her car up on payday and buying a pack of gum, Marcus got everything else…or actually, P.I.G. did.

"Come on, now. I ain't got all day," Marcus called behind him as he leapt from the car.

"I ain't 'bout to go up there wit' that nasty man," she said forcefully.

Marcus knew P.I.G. dug his girl, and he knew he was a little more generous in her presence. "Come on, baby. Ima get some soft for you," he said, leading the way.

She recognized the statement as a command and meekly

complied. Besides, she did like the feeling a couple of lines gave her.

P.I.G. was posted up in his custom-made recliner that was situated next to the front window, where he could monitor the comings and goings of the neighborhood. He was nosey like that. He almost squealed with delight as he watched Tiffany approach the house. He quickly ordered that the sofa nearest him be cleared so she would have to sit close to him. "Well, well, well. What do we have here?" P.I.G. sang as Earl let the young couple in.

Tiffany fought a wave of nausea that swept through her small body as P.I.G. ran his reptilian eyes all over her. She self-consciously tugged at her short skirt in a feeble attempt to shield herself from his lustful glare.

"Have a seat," P.I.G. offered, pointing to the recently abandoned loveseat directly across from him. "What can I do for you, my boy Marcus?" he said genially. A stranger would have thought them to be the best of friends.

"I need a little hard for myself and a gram of soft for my ol' lady," Marcus replied, patting Tiffany's exposed thigh as he spoke. "I ain't got but fifty on me right now," he added, giving her firm thigh a squeeze, "but I got more coming later."

"Of course you do," P.I.G. said with a chuckle. "Not a question, 'specially since you brought this lovely thing with you." He was literally drooling as he stared at Tiffany's dark thighs, making her even more uncomfortable.

Blast had had enough, and she sucked her teeth as she stormed off. She couldn't take any more of her man ogling the young girl and pretending to like Marcus. Truth be told, the only reason Marcus was allowed to come around was because of P.I.G.'s loyalty to his uncle, who got caught with three of P.I.G.'s kilos and took it like a man—all twenty years.

"Earl, go on and serve them up," P.I.G. said, never averting his gaze from Tiffany's legs, not even to blink. He began rocking back and forth as a massive erection grew in his pants. P.I.G. was a pedophile on the low, but he hadn't been able to get a hold of a child as of yet. It wasn't like he wasn't trying, but no matter how much money he offered, nobody seemed to be able to find one for him to have his way with. Tiffany's small frame, although shapely, reminded him of a child and drove him wild. P.I.G.'s rocking increased, and if Earl hadn't come back when he did, he would have let one go in his pants.

"Here ya go," Earl said, tossing the drugs to Marcus.

Marcus wasted no time in breaking off a piece and loading it into his shooter.

Tiffany was amazed and slightly repulsed at how quickly he moved. She watched as he became mesmerized as he twisted and turned the pipe, sucking feverishly. She wondered again if Marcus was becoming a junkie as the drug sizzled under the flame.

"Go on, precious. That stuff ain't gonna snort itself," P.I.G. urged teasingly.

"Sure ain't," the drug seemed to say, causing Tiffany to do a double-take.

I'm tripping. She laughed inwardly as she opened the package. She made two small, neat lines on the glass table and bent forward to inhale them.

P.I.G. bent forward as well to peek down the top of her shirt as she snorted the drug.

She saw him but disregarded it as the powerful drug invaded her senses. *Look all ya want. You'll never get close enough to even smell this coochie,* she laughed to herself as she leaned back to enjoy the rush.

P.I.G. misunderstood, thinking she was smiling at him, and began rocking in his chair again, but Tiffany was again spared the gruesome sights and sounds of P.I.G. cumming on himself by a knock on the door.

"It's ya girl," Earl chuckled as he peered through the peephole in the door. He removed a set of two-by-fours that served as a barrier against the jackers and the crackers and opened the door.

"This bitch," P.I.G. muttered in disgust as Wanda walked in.

"Fuck you, too, nigga," Wanda spat in P.I.G.'s direction. "Gimme a couple eight balls, sweetie," she said to Earl, handing him a hundred-dollar bill.

Earl shot P.I.G. a quick questioning glance before taking the money. When P.I.G. gave a slight nod of his head, he made the sale.

"Go on and take that shit with you," P.I.G. barked when Earl returned with Wanda's package.

"What!? You means I's can take this merchandise off the premises?" Wanda exclaimed sarcastically.

"Yeah, yeah. Take it and get the fuck out," P.I.G. barked.

Marcus, seeing an opportunity to get away and commandeer Tiffany's coke before she had a chance to snort it all, spoke up next. "Say, P.I.G., you mind if we push too? My girl gotta go to work," he asked wistfully.

"Yeah, go on!" P.I.G. barked, grunting as he hoisted his huge frame from his perch. "Matter fact, everybody get the fuck out!" he said, waddling his way to the back room.

Back in the car, Marcus demanded the rest of Tiffany's blow before she could close her door.

"Nooo, baybeee!" Tiffany whined in protest. They both

had plans for the paltry amount, and Tiffany made a mock protest, even though she'd already split it in half as soon as she got it. She knew Marcus well enough to know he would make a play for her dope as well, and as usual, Marcus won her over.

CHAPTER 5

Tiffany was hard at work behind her register in the large department store located in the South Dekalb Mall. Even though it had been a relatively slow day, Tiffany simply could not concentrate. The small amount of cocaine in her purse kept her distracted, as if it was calling her name. Several times during her shift, she'd turned sharply, swearing she heard her name whispered.

"Okay, you win," she finally said to her purse as she picked it up. "You want me to snort you, Ima short you," she told the blow reassuringly as she headed to the restroom.

Relieved to see the employee break room empty, she rushed into a stall to retrieve her stash. Using a manicured pinky nail, she quickly shoveled a scoop in each nostril. She intended to only take a light one on one and save the rest for later, but she was powerless to stop herself as she inhaled the rest. Before she knew it, she was licking the empty tinfoil. Then Tiffany felt a sense of urgency as she stared down into the empty package. She only had two hours left on her shift, but she was far too anxious to stand around with no blow.

Having no choice in the matter, she headed to Mrs.

Lovejoy's office to inform her boss she'd be leaving early for the day. She attempted to concoct a plausible story for her urgent departure, but her mind was still blank as she knocked on the door. Tiffany entered when prompted and stood in front of Mrs. Lovejoy's large desk.

"Oh my God!" the supervisor exclaimed at the sight of Tiffany. "Please sit down, Tiffany. Are you ill?"

"Huh?" Tiffany asked in confusion. "Oh, yeah…ill," she said as her mind caught up. "Must be something I ate," she added, taking a seat.

"You look a mess, child. Do you want me to call your mama?" she asked, concerned.

"No!!!" Tiffany shouted, startling the elderly woman. "I mean, uh…no. I'll be okay. I can drive myself," she said.

"Okay, dear, take the rest of the day," Mrs. Lovejoy said before going into her home remedies for upset stomach.

Tiffany didn't hear a word after "…rest of the day," for as soon as it was uttered, she sprang from the chair and hustled out the door.

She cursed to herself as she walked through the parking lot, past where her car should be parked and headed for the bus stop. "Bet if it was payday, that nigga would have his ass here," she fumed. Since it was Wednesday and her paycheck was long gone, Marcus would be hard to find.

Tiffany cursed again as she scrambled to find correct change as the bus neared. She hated taking public transportation. The buses were always full of weirdoes. She scanned the bus for an empty seat as she paid the fare. She was relieved to find one in the middle of the bus, away from the loudmouthed young goons in the back seats. She could never understand why, after Ms. Parks's noble struggle and all the boycotts and demands to be allowed to sit wherever a person wanted regardless of color, some blacks still flocked to the rear. *Dumb niggas probably think Rosa Parks has swings*, she thought.

Marcus's phone went straight to voicemail again, indicating it was still turned off. Tiffany fought to keep her composure as she prepared to leave yet another message. "Hey, boo. I'm off. I need you to come get me please," she said sweetly, in complete contradiction to what she was really feeling. She felt like screaming, *"Nigga, bring me my fucking car!"* but she knew better. As of late, Marcus had gotten more and more aggressive, to the point of yelling and grabbing on her when he got mad. She wondered if it would escalate to him actually hitting her. "Humph. My daddy didn't even put his hands on me," she said indignantly at the thought.

Without any prompting from her brain, Tiffany's hand reached up and pulled the cord as the bus approached the intersection of Glenwood and Candler Roads. She was on full autopilot as she boarded the 107 bus toward Moreland Avenue…toward P.I.G.'s place.

Tiffany ignored the cat calls from the thugs on the back of the bus. However, the total lack of attention didn't' deter one of the wannabe players from approaching her.

"What it do, shawty?" he slurred, then made a grimace intended to showcase his mouthful of gold teeth.

For a reply, Tiffany frowned and turned back to watch as the depressing ghetto landscape passed by.

"You ain't all dat lil bitch," the dejected mack spat before heading back to his jeering comrades. "Bitch a dyke, y'all!" he said loudly in an attempt to explain why she wasn't interested in him.

Again, she pulled the cord, signaling her stop, and she got off the bus when it came to a hissing stop.

She felt a confusing mix of emotion as she neared P.I.G.'s house. *Girl, what are you doing?* she asked herself as she marched up the sidewalk. She half-hoped Marcus would pull up, but at the same time, she hoped he wouldn't.

P.I.G. blinked a few times to make sure he was seeing correctly. "Get the door!" he shouted excitedly when he realized he wasn't tripping. Tiffany was there…alone!

His sudden outburst caused everyone to look expectantly at the door. When Tiffany walked in, all the smokers went back to smoking—all except Blast. She sucked her teeth, gathered up her work, and headed to the rear.

"Keep it up, you gon' suck one of them teeth right out ya gums!" P.I.G. teased after her. He loved the fact that she was jealous over him. He turned to Tiffany. "Hey, pretty lil thang! What brings you around?" he asked, even though he knew full well why she was there. He saw how much she enjoyed snorting her little lines. He saw her cuff a little of the drug each time she and Marcus came by. Marcus was far too busy sucking on that pipe of his to realize his girl was getting hooked…and fast.

"I was…um…looking for Marcus," she stammered, scanning the room as if she may have missed him.

"I ain't seen him since last night, but I'll tell 'im ya came by," P.I.G. said, nodding to Earl.

On cue, Earl began to reach for the door, causing a slight panic in Tiffany.

"Damn. He got my car," she whined, "and I wanted to get a little something."

"You know your money is good here, lil mama. What you tryina spend?" P.I.G. inquired sweetly.

In the same whiney voice, Tiffany explained that Marcus had her money as well.

"Okay. Well, y'all come back once you catch up with him," P.I.G. said, nodding at Earl again.

"That could be all night. He said he was gonna come here," Tiffany whined.

P.I.G. knew the ball was in his court, but he still had to move slow. He didn't want to scare her off, but he had to get her acclimated to this part of the game. "Well…I was gonna set something out after the show," he said haltingly. "You can stay and get you a few lines if you want."

Tiffany sat down on the nearest sofa as a reply. This time, when she saw P.I.G. gawking at her exposed thighs, she didn't mind. She looked at the two well-dressed men in the room and wondered what kind of show could be forthcoming.

"Well, y'all get into it, Julian," P.I.G. ordered, grabbing his camera.

Julian was a married man with four kids and a nice home in one of Atlanta's outlying counties. Maintaining his family took all of his income, so to maintain his drug habit, he would put on shows for P.I.G. from time to time.

The other man, Tracy, also had a family, but he was such a slave to his sexual desires that there was almost anything he wouldn't do. For him, it was completely sexual, and the drugs were just extra fringe benefits. He was in it to get off.

When both men began to undress, a look of horror spread across Tiffany's face. She understood what was about to go down.

P.I.G. noticed her unease and had to think quick so he wouldn't lose her. "Earl, bring our guest some of that soft," P.I.G. ordered, setting the large man in obedient motion.

Earl rushed from the room, as he himself did not want to see the show either. He returned to drop off the blow and then went back to hang out with Blast in the rear.

Tiffany gasped and turned her head when Julian began performing oral sex on Tracy, but the image was displayed across P.I.G.'s huge screen. Although mortified, she couldn't take her eyes off them. It was like passing a bad car accident; she really didn't want to see the carnage, but she couldn't help but look. Even with the pile of cocaine in front of her, Tiffany's eyes were glued to the men.

They took turns giving each other blow jobs until P.I.G. ordered them to fuck.

Luckily for Tiffany, the blow whispered her name and broke the trance. *"Hey, you!"*

Tiffany smiled at the white powder before she divided it into snortable lines.

She and the men finished about the same time. They dressed and sat back on the sofa like nothing happened.

P.I.G. called for Earl and ordered him to set out an eight ball of crack as payment. "And bring a couple grams for our guest," he added, much to Tiffany's delight. "You can take that with you, lil mama. No telling when you're gonna catch up with that little man of yours," P.I.G. said sweetly.

Just as Tiffany stood to leave, there was a knock on the door.

Earl chuckled as he peeked through the hole, then began the process of opening the door.

"Hey, Earl! Hey, girl!" Wanda sang cheerfully as she walked in. She and Tiffany had spoken briefly over the past few weeks, whenever they happened to be there at the same time. They talked about girls' stuff like hair and nails…over hits of cocaine. "Bring me a couple of eight balls, sweetie," Wanda told Earl, making a big show of ignoring P.I.G. "So, what are you doing over here, girl?" Wanda asked Tiffany.

"Looking for my man and my car," Tiffany replied in sista

gurl mode, with her hand on her hip, her head moving, and her eyes rolling.

"You need a ride?" Wanda offered.

"Y'all know I don't like nobody taking my shit up outta here," P.I.G. interjected. As much as he hated Wanda speaking to him, her ignoring him bothered him even more.

"Nigga, ain't nobody tryina hear that fuck shit you talking!" Wanda spat. "Much business my man bring yo' fat ass," she threw in for good measure.

That did the trick and humbled P.I.G., because Wanda was right. Mike was an important man who was feared and respected. P.I.G. hated Wanda with his whole black, overworked heart, but business was business.

After Earl served her, Wanda left with young Tiffany in tow.

P.I.G. was in a foul mood and needed to take it out on someone. "Get over here, Julian!" P.I.G. ordered, pulling out his huge penis.

Diache sighed as he put his pipe down and complied.

Better him than me. Tracy laughed to himself, happy to be sucking on a pipe instead of P.I.G.

* * *

Damn! Stripping must pay good, Tiffany thought as she followed Wanda into her small house.

The two-bedroom cottage was located on Wylie Street, in Atlanta's Cabbage Town section. That area, like many others in the city, was changing rapidly. Houses were being bought and sold on a daily basis. Some were razed and rebuilt almost overnight.

Wanda's house had a "For Sale" sign out front as well. It

was owned by her boyfriend Mike, who was looking to add to his fortune. It had quadrupled in value since he'd purchased it, so the time was ripe to sell.

"Have a seat," Wanda offered, waving a diamond-laden hand toward a plush blue leather sectional sofa that dominated the small room.

Tiffany took in all the rich accouterments as she sat down. The carpet was incredibly thick, swallowing most of Tiffany's sandal. It was a shade darker than the sofa, creating a nice contrast. The room was embellished with glass and chrome, and a huge fish tank filled with several exotic creatures filled an entire wall. "I love your place," Tiffany said emphatically.

"Thank you, girl. Courtesy of them trick-ass niggas at the club," Wanda said as she dumped the guts out of a blunt and went on. "I still can't understand how they pay so much money just to look at some coochie. They be in the streets all day, taking penitentiary chances, sellin' dope, robbin', and killing, just to throw it at a bitch." She laughed. As she laced a blunt with cocaine, she continued, "I mean, then them niggas be showing off, tryina outdo each other, talking 'bout they makin' it rain. Nigga, please!" Wanda laughed again. "God make it rain. Y'all niggas is tricks. We be like, 'Yeah, Daddy, make it rain,'" she said, stopping to light the blunt.

The room grew silent as Wanda lit it. The heavy dose of crack sizzled loudly under the flame.

Tiffany caught herself staring and quickly snapped out of it. "So how much y'all be making up in there?" Tiffany asked, totally ignoring all the rules of grammar in order to sound hip.

"It depends," Wanda said between gulps of air. "'Bout a stack on a regular night, two or three on a good one."

"A thousand dollars!?" Tiffany exclaimed in disbelief.

"To…just to dance? But I could never take my clothes off in front of all those men," she said, looking repulsed.

"Shit! Y'all young hoes be doin' the same shit in a regular club," Wanda retorted, slightly offended. "Letting them niggas dry hump on y'all till they bust in they pants. Shit. Ain't 'nare a nigga getting no free nut off me," she said, calming back down.

"I know that's right," Tiffany added, embarrassed by the inadvertent insult.

"Mmhmm, girl," Wanda said, extending the blunt to Tiffany.

"Uh-uh," Tiffany replied, shaking her head, terrified.

"Scared? You scared?" Wanda laughed before hitting the blunt again.

Scared to death! Tiffany thought to herself.

CHAPTER 6

"What...the...fuck!?" Marcus groaned loudly as the incessant noise grew louder. "Fucking bad-ass kids," he fumed, realizing that the source of the offending noise was one of his nephews bouncing a ball against the wall in the next room. He covered his head with his pillow, trying in vain to drown out the sound. When that didn't work, Marcus began to mentally plan his day. The plan was simple: *Get high*. The only issue at hand was how.

His thoughts drifted to Tiffany as he felt his morning erection throb. "Damn, I ain't hit that in a minute," he reflected as he began slowly stroking himself. It wasn't as if he'd lost interest in Tiffany, but trying to stay high consumed most of his time, most of his energy, and all of his money—which was really hers in the first place. He became slightly embarrassed at the memory of their last sexual encounter. He'd been smoking crack for hours before Tiffany arrived at the hotel and couldn't get an erection to save his life.

Tiffany had enjoyed the extended foreplay, of course, but she was shocked when she reached down to guide him inside of her and found him uncharacteristically limp. "What's wrong with you!?" she shrieked at the touch of his flaccid penis.

"Ain't shit wrong with me," he shot back defensively, as if she were the problem. "Let a nigga get a little head," Marcus demanded.

"Boy, stop." Tiffany chuckled. They'd only had sex a handful of times since she'd finally given it up on prom night a few months prior. She'd made it clear that oral sex either way was out of the question.

Nevertheless, Marcus persisted, and an argument ensued. After getting thoroughly cursed out, Tiffany left in a huff. No sooner than she did, Marcus paid a junkie for a blow job. As of late, that was the only sex he was getting.

Marcus stroked himself until he released onto his own stomach. He used a nearby T-shirt to clean himself off and then tossed it on the floor. He was still shuddering from the climax when he reached for his phone. "What it do, shawty?" he said gruffly into it. His voice was still strained, as they were the first words he'd uttered for the day.

"Who dis?" Tiffany replied, groggy herself from just waking up.

"Fuck you mean, 'Who dis'?" Marcus snapped. "Bitch, how many niggas be calling you?"

"Bitch!?" Tiffany exclaimed in disbelief, reeling as if she'd been slapped.

Marcus knew he'd gone too far and was about to try and straighten it out, but there was no one on the line to apologize to. "Shit," he cursed to himself as he hit the redial button. He expected the call to go directly to voicemail, but to his surprise, Tiffany answered on the first ring, flying into a tirade.

"First of all, nigga, I ain't nobody's bitch," Tiffany began. Knowing it would be prudent to let her blow off some steam, Marcus sat with the phone on his chest while she vented. "I love you," he said sweetly once the vibrations on his chest slowed, signaling the end of her rant.

"I can't tell," Tiffany responded calmly as the magic word instantly took effect.

"I heard P.I.G. broke you off real nice last night. I know you saved some fo' ya man," Marcus said, smiling through the phone line.

"I ain't got nothing left," Tiffany lied as her eyes instinctively shot to her purse, where the remnants of last night's package were.

"Come on now, lil mama," Marcus urged. "My nigga Pony told me P.I.G. threw you in an extra eight ball."

Tiffany wondered silently if nosey-ass Pony told him he'd asked for some pussy. P.I.G. did indeed break her off after she watched another of his sordid shows. A wannabe local rapper called Chieva let Julian suck him off for some coke. P.I.G. taped it, demanding that he *meow* like a kitten as he got his salad tossed. The dude had the audacity to try and holla at Tiffany once they were done.

"Ain't none left. Me and Wanda snorted it all," Tiffany said.

"Wanda!? Bitch, fuck you doing with that bitch?" Marcus spat as his anger began to build. He didn't like Wanda either, especially after she laughed in his face when he hit on her. More than anything, he was pissed to have to start his quest to get high from ground zero.

"Bitch? Really? Again?" Tiffany asked as if she hadn't heard correctly.

"Yeah, I said 'bitch', bitch," Marcus answered. "Dumb-ass bitch, ho bitch, stupid-ass bitch…" was all he could get out before the line went dead. He called back and called her a few more bitch names on her voicemail—every kind of bitch known to man, plus two he made up on his own.

Marcus looked around his room and cursed its sparseness. It looked like he'd been robbed. In fact, he had been; he'd robbed himself for drug money. Gone was his TV, DVD player, and his stereo. His Xbox, his PlayStation, and hundreds of games were up in smoke. The jewelry he once wore had long been smoked away.

Hearing his older sister Debbie finally order her son to stop playing ball in the house, Marcus decided to try his luck with her. He realized it was futile to ask his sister for money, but he was a crackhead, and his entire existence was an exercise in futility anyway. *At least ten dollars,* he reasoned to himself as he slid into the filthy jeans he had peeled off only hours before. Then he picked up the disgusting wadded T-shirt, complete with drying semen, and put it on as well.

"Hey, Uncle Marcus," his six-year-old nephew greeted cheerfully as he passed him in the hallway.

Marcus grunted a reply and patted the child on his head.

His other nephew, five-year-old Dontavious, just sneered at him. He wasn't feeling him one bit after their Nintendo mysteriously walked up out the house.

"I don't fuck with you either, lil nigga," Marcus grumbled as he passed the glaring child.

"Uh oh, Mama, hide yo' purse. There go that junkie," Debbie chided as Marcus entered the kitchen.

"The village whore speaks," Marcus chuckled as he hugged his mother and kissed her face.

Only unconditional mother's love prevented her from being repulsed by the smell of filth and semen emanating from Marcus. "I know y'all better watch y'all mouth in my house," their mother warned.

"But, Mama, he really is a junkie."

"But, Mama, she really is a ho," Marcus replied, mocking his sister's tone.

"I swear y'all gon' be the death of me," their mother said solemnly.

"We just playin', Mama. See?" Marcus said, hugging his sister and attempting to kiss her face.

"Eww! Get off me, boy. I don't know where your lips been," Debbie squealed, trying to fend off her brother's kisses. She loved her little brother with her whole heart—the same heart that was breaking as she watched him destroy himself, powerless to stop him. Debbie had already witnessed drugs destroy her first two baby daddies. The first smoked himself into a fatal cardiac arrest. The second got himself murdered trying to sell on a block that wasn't his to sell on.

As much as Debbie loved Marcus, he loved her more. It pained him when she earned a bad reputation back in school. Always a pretty girl, her pudgy frame killed her self-esteem. Once word got out that she put out, the guys flocked around, the girls gossiped, and her name was sullied. Debbie had always been a big girl, and then she kept an extra twenty pounds after each of her sons was born. Since even good pussy has its limits, guys stopped coming around once she tilted the scales at 250.

Debbie and Marcus's mother, Sister Jones, was a hardworking, hard-praying, deeply religious woman. Again, unconditional mother's love caused her to ignore her children's shortcomings. She knew Marcus was an addict, just like his father was. She knew her daughter was promiscuous, just like she herself was back in the day. Now Jesus was the only man in her life. She knew He had saved her and could save her wayward children if she could only get them to darken the door and warm the pews of the church.

As soon as their mother went to the dining room and was safely out of earshot, Marcus cracked on his sister for money. "Say, shawty, let a nigga hol' something till later?" he asked with a chuckle, even though he was dead serious. The laugh was a self-defense mechanism in case he got shot down. That way, he could claim he was just playing without looking like a fool.

"Nigga, you must already be high if you think Ima give you some money," Debbie said and laughed loudly.

"Come on, sis. Just ten bucks?" he pleaded desperately.

"Just like you gon' replace the boys' game that walked up outta here?" Debbie said loudly.

"I done told you I ain't take that, but I got some money coming—"

"Yeah, I know. 'Later'!" Debbie laughed. "Nigga, I wouldn't give you ten cent to put cheese on a Checkers burger, so you know I ain't 'bout to give you ten dollars to give to the dope man," she added, becoming indignant.

"What y'all fussing about now?" their mother asked as she entered the kitchen.

"He beggin' for money again," Debbie snitched.

"Money!?" Sister Jones said in mock surprise. "Boy, if you want some money, then go back to work."

"Soon, Mama, soon. Things a little slow right now," Marcus lied. Truth be told, Marcus couldn't handle both working and getting high, so the job had to go. Besides, Tiffany had a job to support him and his habit.

His mother shook her head as her mind flashed to all the ongoing construction projects she passed every day on her commute to and from work. "Well, come to the church with me sometime, and things will turn around," she said wistfully.

"Come on, Debbie. Just ten bucks?" Marcus begged, ignoring his mother's comment.

"Nigga...oops, sorry, Mama. Boy, I gotta spend at least thirty dollars on taxis taking these kids to Walmart, then DFCS, then ShopBrite," Debbie said.

Jackpot! Marcus screamed inside his head. He had Tiffany's car outside, and he was sure he could get all that money. "Give me the money, and I'll run you wherever you gotta go," he announced with his hand extended.

Debbie tried to decline, but Mama wasn't hearing it. "Let your brother drive you, and give him twenty dollars," she demanded, knowing it would prevent someone's property from being stolen...or at least delay it.

As Marcus loaded his niece and carseat into the car, his mind was racing. He was desperately trying to formulate a plot to get the money first, so he cold get a blast. "You gotta pay me first," Marcus demanded once they were all inside.

"Yeah, right." Debbie laughed. "You ain't getting a dime until me and my kids are safely back home."

Marcus set off for their first stop, ignoring the low fuel light. Even when it began beeping, he intended to ignore the warning.

"Boy, you ain't got no gas!" Debbie exclaimed once she noticed it.

"We straight," Marcus said, forging ahead.

"Straight...hell, boy, pull over ahead and get some gas," she demanded.

"Uh-uh. I ain't spending my money on no gas fo' this car," Marcus said plainly.

"Man, I'll pay for it," Debbie said ruefully.

Marcus was calculating how to make the most of the

twenty bucks he had coming. He didn't want any of the bullshit he might find on the street, and he knew he couldn't see P.I.G. with that paltry amount unless he was planning on sucking dick, which he wasn't. *That nigga will have you sweeping up.* He laughed at himself as he pumped the gas. *I'll figure something out*, he vowed.

Three hours later, Marcus was following his sister through the aisle of Walmart, pushing a cart. While she picked out cheap outfits and shoes for her kids, Marcus scanned the store for something to steal. Inspiration struck him when the Electronics Department came into view. "Here, lil man," Marcus said, giving control of the shopping cart to his nephew. He paced the section, scoping out DVDs and iPods. The busy clerk paid him no attention as he began to load up. It got so good that Marcus snatched the tags off a small tote bag and filled it with loot. He actually got an erection as he stuffed the bag with merchandise. The high-ticket items were locked in a display case, but he still had hundreds of dollars worth of items. "Be easy," he told himself as he made his way to the front. "Almost there," he said reassuringly as the exit door came into view. He held his breath as he walked past the sensors. To his relief, there were no alarms, no guards, no problems.

Marcus had done a lot of foul shit since he began smoking, and he felt nothing—no guilt or shame—most of the time. He did, however, feel a tinge of remorse as he pulled out of the Walmart parking lot, leaving his sister and her children stranded there. "At least she can keep the twenty," he told his reflection, as if that made everything alright.

CHAPTER 7

It was another typical hot, humid summer day in the South. Tiffany thanked God and then her father for the ice-cold air conditioner that cooled the house as she did her household chores. After running the vacuum through the entire house, she went to work dusting and polishing. She felt a sense of pride and gratitude for the nice home her father had provided for his family.

"Hey, girl," Tiffany beamed at her mother, who was hard at work herself; she always whipped up a big brunch as the family did their weekend chores, and today's consisted of scrambled eggs, bacon, home fries, and biscuits.

"Almost ready, dear," her mother replied, returning the cheerful smile.

"Good, cuz I'm starvin' like Marvin." Tiffany chuckled as she snagged a slice of crispy bacon.

"'Bout time you ate something, girl. You been hurtin' my feelings lately, turning ya nose up at my food," she slipped in. She'd been looking for an opportunity to address her daughter's recent lack of appetite.

"Gurl, you know I love ya cooking," Tiffany sang,

grabbing a hot biscuit to prove the point. She chomped into the biscuit as she headed up to her room. "Call me when it's ready!" Tiffany called behind her.

As Tiffany neared her room, she heard the phone ringing. The D-lite ringtone always made her want to dance. By the time she fished the phone out, it had stopped ringing. "Shit!" she proclaimed at the missed call. She didn't particularly want to speak with Marcus, but she wanted her car back.

Just as she was about to dial the phone, a folded-up bill in her purse caught her attention. *"Psst..."* it seemed to say.

She debated on whether or not she should take a hit for two whole seconds before digging in. A few seconds after she began, the bill was empty. She lay back to enjoy her buzz, just as her mother's voice drifted upstairs. Since her appetite had vanished, she decided to ignore her mother's beckoning. She shook her head at the half-eaten biscuit on the nightstand.

"Tiff, don't you hear your mother?" her father asked, sticking his head inside the partially open door.

"Don't you know how to knock?" she replied curtly at the intrusion.

"Excuse me, young lady?" her father said in disbelief, a look of pure confusion pasted on his face.

"I'm sorry, Daddy," Tiffany whined, using the little girl voice that always proved effective when dealing with her father. "I was about to change. You embarrassed me," she added. She knew she had her daddy wrapped around her finger, but maintaining that required the utmost respect.

Her father doted on his wife and daughter, and he worked long and hard to provide them with a good life. The house and the cars were a testament of his accomplishments as a provider. It was a far cry from the path he almost took in the streets.

He glanced out Tiffany's window to decide if he should wash the cars and noticed that hers wasn't there…again. "Girl, where is your car?" he asked sternly.

"Um…Marcus had a job interview early today," she lied. She knew full well that a job would have to come looking for Marcus, and even if one found him, it would have to beg him to take it.

"I don't like that boy keeping your car," he said slowly. "I bought that car for you, not for him."

"I know, Daddy, but once he finds another job, he'll be able to get him another one," she said, fighting her own frustration. She didn't like him keeping her car any more than her father did, and she was getting sick of defending her lazy, leeching boyfriend.

"Yeah, well, speaking of cars," her father said, taking a seat on her bed, "the insurance agent called me and said your payment is late. They're about to cancel your policy."

"Shit!" Tiffany exclaimed. "Oops. I mean…shoot. I got that money order last week and ain't mailed it out yet."

"Last month, you mean," her father corrected.

"Ima send it out today," Tiffany said, easing back into baby girl mode.

"Okay, sweetheart," he said, rising from the bed. "Come on down and get some of the food ya mama hooked up."

"Y'all go 'head. I'm not hungry," Tiffany replied.

"Oh?" her father asked. His wife had spoken to him about their daughter's recent change in appetite. She hadn't lost any weight that he could tell, but his wife was worried about it.

"Yeah, my stomach hurts. I think my period is coming," she said, knowing that would get him out of there.

It did the trick, and her father rushed out of the room. "I'll tell your mama to put you a plate in the oven for later," he said over his shoulder.

Tiffany's mind flashed back to drugs. She cursed herself for giving Marcus all her money. Payday was only the day before, and she didn't have a dime left—no money for gas, no money for her insurance, and worst of all, no money for blow. She had no idea where her next gram was coming from.

She tried Marcus, but the call went straight to voicemail, so she left him a message. "Nigga, bring me MY car," she said hotly after the tone.

* * *

"Hey, baby, you feeling better?" Tiffany's mother inquired when she entered the kitchen.

"A little," she said, holding her head. "Migraine, I think."

"Ya daddy said your tummy is hurting," her mother asked.

"Oh, yeah. That too," she replied, reminded of the lie she'd told. She was trying to figure out the best approach to separate her mother from some of her money.

"Well, I put a plate in the microwave," her mother said as she went back to her task of loading the dishwasher.

"I ain't hungry," she replied, causing her mother to pause from her chore.

"Girl, something ain't right with you," she said, placing the back of her hand against her daughter's forehead.

Knowing there was no fever to find, Tiffany pulled away from her mother's touch. "I'll grab a bite to eat at work…if I make it," she said pitifully, setting the stage for a loan.

"Yeah, ya daddy told me that boy got your car again," her mother said, with displeasure clear in her voice. She and her husband had once been very fond of Marcus, but now he was just "that boy."

"Mmmhmm. Plus, I done messed around and ain't paid my insurance. Daddy gon' kill me," Tiffany said sadly.

"Didn't you just get paid?" her mother asked sharply.

"Yes, ma'am, but I had a lot of bills to pay," Tiffany replied.

"Bills!?" Her mother chuckled. "What bills *you* got?"

"Um…let's see. Hair, nails, clothes, cell phone, clothes… and oh, yeah…clothes," Tiffany joked, appealing to her mother's sense of fashion and vanity.

"Girl, I swear, you gon' break me," her mother replied, reaching for her purse. "How much you need?"

Tiffany did some quick math in her head before answering. *Go for an eight ball, twenty for gas, and ten for nails.* "I think $200 should do it," she sang.

"Two hundred!?" Tiffany's mother exclaimed. "Chile, what you need so much money for?"

"Seventy for insurance, twenty for gas, ten for lunch, and the rest to hold me through the week," she said evenly.

"I'll tell you what. Ima give you $100 and send a check for your insurance, but you gon' have to eat something first," she replied.

"Okay," Tiffany huffed, plopping stubbornly into a chair. She tried to eat, but it was as if her throat was closed. No matter how much she chewed, it took a swig of juice to get the food down. "I'm full, Mama," Tiffany whined halfway through her plate.

Knowing she'd deliberately overloaded the plate, her mother was satisfied with the effort.

Tiffany took off like a shot once she had the money in her hand. "Thanks, Mama!" she yelled as she hit the stairs, taking them two at a time.

* * *

Tiffany had lost her buzz because of the heavy brunch, but the anticipation of that next package boosted her spirits. Just the thought of a hit made her stomach churn.

Before sitting on the toilet, she turned on the shower so it could be at the desired temperature when she got in. After relieving herself, Tiffany stepped out of her clothes and into the shower. There, she removed the handheld showerhead from its cradle and directed the water onto her backside to make sure she was thoroughly clean. The steam of the water sent a vibration through her entire body as it licked at her vagina. Tiffany adjusted the flow to pulsate and applied it directly on her now-throbbing vagina. Using her free hand, she spread her outer lips for direct clitoral stimulation. In seconds, she let out a shriek as her body convulsed from her first orgasm.

Her legs were still shaking as she stood in front of her mirror to dress. Feeling sexy, she selected a white thong and bra set, for starters. "That nigga tripping," she sad aloud as she admired her figure. She had been feeling a little self-conscious lately since Marcus showed no interest in her. "Ain't nothing wrong with me," she said, remembering his lack of erection at their last encounter.

Tiffany shook her head at the plain outfit she'd laid out on the bed. It had been selected with the bus ride in mind, comfort being paramount. Having a change in plans, she pulled out a sexy miniskirt and a matching top. "Somebody gonna gimme a ride," she mused to herself as she dressed. A comfortable pair of sandals completed the ensemble, and she was set.

Once outside, Tiffany slipped on her shades and took off in

the direction of the bus stop, knowing full well she wouldn't be taking any buses. She hadn't walked half a block before a car honked its horn behind her. She smiled to herself, pleased with the attention, and then put a little extra sway in her hips, pretending to ignore the car.

"Girl, get in this car," the driver demanded as he pulled alongside her.

Tiffany was embarrassed and pleased when she turned and saw who it was. She and Carlos lived across the street from each other and had grown up together. Despite their close proximity, they rarely saw each other lately.

"Hey, lo," Tiffany said sweetly as she slid into the passenger seat.

"Hey, yourself. Why you walking like that? What, you broke yo' hip?" he teased.

"Boy, stop." She giggled, fastening her seatbelt.

"You lookin' good, Tiff," Carlos remarked, staring at her black thighs.

When he pulled away from the curb, Tiffany gave him a quick once-over as well. *Damn, you looking good yourself,* she thought as she took in the muscles straining against his T-shirt. She admired his smooth chocolate skin tone, remembering how that had been a determining factor in her choosing Marcus over him so many years earlier. She still hated her own dark skin, but his looked good! *What a mistake that was,* she admitted to herself.

Tiffany and Carlos were very close growing up, even sharing their first kiss at seven. They planned to get married when they got older…but then they got older.

She glanced up at Carlos's freshly cut hair, sporting ring after ring of waves. He was in college, earning a business degree, and still running his own business—a landscaping business he had started in the ninth grade by cutting lawns on their block. Now he had ten employees, three trucks, and equipment. *Damn, I played myself,* Tiffany admitted again as she finally accepted the fact that Marcus was a bum.

"Hellooo?" Carlos sang, jolting her back to the present. "Where to, shawty?" he joked, using slang that sounded odd coming from him.

"Um, I gotta go to work, but can I make a quick stop?" she asked sweetly.

"Anything for you," he said flirtatiously. "Lead the way." He followed the turn-by-turn directions Tiffany gave him as he drove, stealing glances at his sexy passenger every chance he got. "Say, where your car at?" Carlos inquired as they rode.

"My man got it. He got a new job," Tiffany lied. She stifled a smile as she watched his jaw tighten at the mention of Marcus, her so-called man.

Tiffany knew Carlos hated her boyfriend. They almost came to blows over her back in the eleventh grade. Even though Carlos stood almost a full foot taller than Marcus, he still stepped to him about their friendship. It was Marcus's contention that since she was his girl, their friendship had to end. The only thing that kept Carlos from whipping his ass was a slight, almost imperceptible shake of Tiffany's head. Marcus foolishly thought he had scared the larger man into backing down, and to this day, he was certain Carlos was afraid of him.

The mention of Marcus seemed to foul the mood between the two old friends, and they rode in silence for a while. Tiffany unconsciously rubbed at her nose, which had been bothering her more and more lately. It seemed like it was always stopped up, as if it was full of boogers. She discreetly slid a pinky nail in her nostril in an attempt to clear it. In the process, she scratched off a scab, causing a small rivulet of blood to trickle out.

Carlos sucked his teeth loudly, shaking his head, dismayed by the obvious.

"Fuck you shakin' ya head fo'?" Tiffany asked indignantly.

"Look at you," he said, disgusted. "I can't believe he got you fucking with that shit too."

"I don't snort no powder," Tiffany shot back, unwittingly telling on herself.

"Whatever, man." Carlos chuckled. "Everyone know ya little boyfriend's a damn junkie. Look like he turning you out too."

"My man ain't no junkie! He got a good job," she said, feebly defending Marcus more out of habit than out of feeling.

"Fuck you, nigga. I just wanted a ride. I ain't tryina hear all dat shit you talkin'. Matter of fact, you can let me out!" Tiffany screamed.

Carlos pulled the car to a stop so quickly she almost got whiplash.

"Wait…" Tiffany pleaded, realizing that he would indeed put her out. "I'm saying though…dang…" she said sweetly, putting her hand on his arm.

Her sweet-talking did the trick, and Carlos pulled back out into traffic.

"I take a little bump every now and then," she purred. "You know…just party a little."

"Ain't no such thing as a recreational cocaine user. That shit is dangerous. You gonna fuck around and end up like Tosha," he said solemnly.

The mention of Tosha was enough to send shivers up Tiffany's spine. She had been the prettiest, most popular girl in the school, if not the city. She began getting high, though, in ninth grade and was strung out by tenth. She was stripping in the eleventh grade, and a prostitute by the time she hit her senior year. She died right before graduation. The number of people she infected directly or indirectly with the HIV that ultimately killed her still grew by the day.

"I think I'm going to talk to your daddy," Carlos said matter-of-factly.

"You do, and Ima tell him you tried to rape me," Tiffany exploded, horrified at the thought of her father finding out about his darling daughter's drug use.

"Rape you?" Carlos laughed. "You'll be out her selling pussy you keep fucking with that shit."

"That's a fucked-up thing to say, Carlos." Tiffany sobbed, unable to prevent the tears from falling.

"I'm sorry, Tiff," Carlos said sincerely. "I love you, man. I don't wanna see you go out bad, that's all."

"Love me?" Tiffany asked, genuinely moved by his words.

"Of course I love you, Tiff. Always have, and I know you love me. You just don't know it," he said, pulling to a stop in front of P.I.G.'s house as directed. He leaned over and took Tiffany into his arms to console the still-crying girl. The hug began platonically, but then Tiffany looked up into his eyes. In an instant, she knew he was right. He did love her, and she loved him.

Just as they drew near to sharing their first kiss since second grade, the door flew open, and she was snatched from the car. "Fuck you doing with this lame-ass nigga!?" Marcus spat so furiously he was drooling. Before she could utter a word in response, she was knocked off her feet by a vicious open-handed slap.

Carlos jerked off his seatbelt to exit the car, but Marcus raced around to the driver side before he could open the door. Marcus pointed a small-caliber pistol in his face and pulled back the hammer. "You want something, fuck nigga?" he growled as his finger tightened around the trigger.

"Naw, you got it." Carlos chuckled as he eased his hand toward the forty-caliber pistol he kept under the armrest. Realizing he probably couldn't get his gun out before Marcus put a couple in his face, he settled back in his seat. "We ain't got no problem," he said.

"That's what the fuck I thought, busta-ass nigga." Marcus laughed. "Now get your punk ass outta here!" he shouted as Carlos pulled away.

"I'll be seeing you, Marcus," Carlos said ominously as he pulled off.

"Whatever." Marcus laughed, making his way back over to where Tiffany was standing. Before she could offer a word of explanation, he slapped her again.

When he reared back for another blow, his friend Pony grabbed his hand.

"You need to stay out my business," Marcus warned his friend, danger evident in his voice.

"Chill, shawty. We out here in front P.I.G.'s. You know he don't stand for no drama over here," Pony warned. As he spoke, he looked Tiffany up and down slowly. He flirted with her every chance he got, even in front of Marcus, who was too busy chasing a blast to notice or care.

The thought of being banned from P.I.G.'s and the best coke in the city knocked all the buck out of Marcus. When he glanced up and saw P.I.G. looking back, a shiver ran up his spine. "Come on," he said contritely, leading the way up the walk.

P.I.G. had witnessed the entire event but wasn't mad. In fact, he was pleased. For one thing, that lovely Tiffany was back, and for another, that silly young nigga was blowing her by the day.

Tiffany shot daggers at Marcus's back as they walked. He missed it, but P.I.G. didn't, and neither did Pony.

CHAPTER 8

Tiffany let out a sigh of relief after completing her last sale of the day. Eight long hours on her feet dealing with rude customers and their fickle demands—and worse, it was eight long hours without a single hit. But the wait was almost over. As soon as she counted out her drawer and straightened her area, she was free to go. The thought of a nice, long line of blow caused her stomach to flutter.

Marcus had given her five counterfeit hundred-dollar bills to switch for real ones. Tiffany still had yet to make the swap and was running out of time. The bills were good and would have even fooled her. She hoped they would fool her boss too. She had initially refused to use her job to exchange the fake bills, reasoning that they could use them to buy the drugs instead. Marcus countered that it would burn his bridges with the dealers, and he'd much rather burn hers at work if it came down to that. It wasn't until he agreed to split the money that she relented. She calculated that she could pay the $100 that was past due on her insurance and still have enough left to get a nice little package.

Paranoia set in as she prepared to commit her first crime.

She was so sure all her co-workers were suddenly watching her. Feeling clever, she decided to make the switch on the elevator up to cash out. Tiffany wasn't aware of the overhead camera in the corner of the elevator, nor was she aware that she was under surveillance. At Mrs. Lovejoy's direction, one of the store detectives had been watching her all day since her receipts had been fifty to sixty dollars short every day as of late.

Even though her back was to the camera when Tiffany made the switch, the observant guard could tell she did something suspicious, and Mrs. Lovejoy was notified of the anomaly.

Tiffany broke out into a cold sweat as she watched Mrs. Lovejoy meticulously count her drawer for the third time. It was all she could do to not take off running or break down and confess.

Her supervisor was concentrating so hard on the count that she missed the fake bills time after time. Satisfied that all the money was there, twelve dollars over, in fact, Mrs. Lovejoy thanked Tiffany and excused her.

Still fearing that the deception would be discovered, Tiffany practically ran from the store. She was relieved to find Marcus parked in her car right outside the exit. Any other day, she might have had to wait for hours for her car, and some days it didn't even come at all.

Marcus sat behind the wheel, wide-eyed, looking every bit the junkie he'd become. Tiffany wondered again what she still saw in him. He had long ago stopped caring about his appearance. His usually well-maintained wavy hair was now an unkempt bush on the top of his head. Once a nice dresser, he now wore the same dingy jeans and shirt daily, like some sort of crackhead uniform.

It was at that moment she decided she was through with Marcus. Mentally, she quit him on the spot. After she got her half of the money, it would be over. Her thoughts were shattered by the blaring of the car horn.

"Bitch, come da fuck on!" Marcus screamed wildly.

Pony, who was riding shotgun, laughed hysterically. "Pimp! Get that nigga, pimp!" he yelled in support.

Tiffany ducked her head in embarrassment and rushed to the car.

Pony leaned forward to allow her to ride in the back of her own car.

She felt some kind of way about it, but she decided to comply. She wasn't in the mood to get cursed out again. She was just thankful none of her co-workers was around to see her get humiliated.

"You got my money?" Marcus demanded before both cheeks even touched the seat.

"*Your* money?" she replied in confusion. "You said we was gonna split it."

"Bitch, I put this shit together. Me! You get what the fuck I give you," Marcus spat angrily.

"Yeah, pimping." Pony chuckled in support.

Too afraid not to, Tiffany reached into her bra and retrieved the money. "Where we going?" Tiffany asked as Marcus bypassed 20 West, which would have been the quickest route to P.I.G.'s house.

Marcus sucked his teeth as a reply, which caused another round of laughter from his assistant pimp.

Pony shot a sideways glance at Marcus before reaching back to rub Tiffany's thigh. "We got a new connect we finna try," he said, reaching for her crotch.

Tiffany let him cop a feel to spite Marcus, but she squeezed her legs together to prevent him from going too far. *Like I really want another damn junkie,* she thought to herself as she pushed his hand away.

Marcus zipped up Candler Road recklessly. He swung a hard left at Krystals, then a quick right onto Hooper Street.

Tiffany knew this was where the bootlegger's house was, and she assumed Marcus intended to buy them some beer. Since they were underage, it was one of the few places where they could buy alcohol. She was always amazed at how an illegal establishment could operate at full blast the way the bootleggers did. One would think they would make some effort at discretion, since they were breaking the law and all.

Marcus pulled to a hard stop a few houses before the bootleggers and jumped out. Pony was close behind like a junkie Tonto. They entered through a side door, returning the same way minutes later. On the way back to the car, Pony stopped and bought a sack of weed from a dude they all went to school with.

"Are we going to P.I.G.'s now?" Tiffany asked, disturbed by the pleading she heard in her own voice.

Marcus, who was obviously above speaking with her, only sucked his teeth. It was one of the many habits Tiffany looked forward to not having to deal with after this night was done.

"We got straight here," Pony replied, growing tired of the attitude himself.

Marcus made a couple of turns and emerged onto Glenwood. After crossing over Candler, he turned into the parking lot of a shabby motel a few blocks later. "Come on," Marcus demanded as he exited the vehicle.

Pony and Tiffany got out and followed him to a room on the second floor. He produced a key and led the way inside.

Tiffany almost gagged from the strong odor emanating from within. It smelled like ass and cigarettes, topped off with stale beer.

Once inside, the men huddled at the small table as Tiffany sat gingerly on the bed. "Shit look straight," Marcus announced as he produced a large bag of crack.

"Fuck what it look like. What it hit like?" Pony exclaimed greedily, with pipe in hand.

"Did y'all get some soft for me?" Tiffany pleaded as the men loaded their shooters.

"All they had was hard," Marcus said without bothering to look back at her.

"Here. Roll you a blunt," Pony said, handing her the weed and a wrap.

"I wanted me a bump too," Tiffany whined desperately.

"Here. Roll yaself a primo," Marcus said, handing a few crumbs her direction.

Tiffany hesitated only for a second before accepting the drugs. She repeated the process she'd seen Wanda perform many times.

Marcus and Pony were engaged in the Crack Olympics, trying to out-smoke each other, so it took a minute for Tiffany to get a light. When she was able to get a lighter from Pony, he quickly snatched it back, trying to catch up with Marcus, who had taken a slight lead in the race to get high.

The blunt sizzled loudly as Tiffany inhaled. The effect was instant and intense. She literally felt her life change at that moment, and she knew her days of snorting cocaine were over. "Pass me a beer," she said giddily between pulls. The blunt was still well above the halfway mark when Tiffany discreetly put it out and hid it in her purse.

"Let's go on and split the rest so I can hit this pussy,"

Marcus suddenly announced.

Tiffany was disgusted by the crassness of the remark, but she was horny enough to let it pass. She was actually amazed how horny she was. *One last time*, she reasoned. *One for the road.*

"You want me to stay and help?" Pony asked as he gathered his supplies.

Marcus shrugged his shoulders as if he didn't care one way or the other.

"Hell, naw, he can't stay," Tiffany said forcefully, looking at the stranger she once loved.

"A'ight, I'm gone. Don't beat it up too bad." Pony laughed on his way out the door.

"Get dem drawers off," Marcus demanded, peeling off his dirty uniform.

Tiffany was surprised he was still insisting on being an asshole with his company gone. He usually only showed his ass when people were around. This was a first…and a last. If she hadn't been so horny, she would have told him right then and there to go fuck himself and then gone home and done the same. But Tiffany removed her clothes as directed and lay back on the bed.

Marcus took one last sizzling blast before climbing on top of her. He blew the smoke in her face, causing her to wince from the tartness of his breath. Still, she inhaled. Marcus grinded himself between her legs as he sucked on her breast.

Far too horny for foreplay, Tiffany reached down to put him inside of her. "Eww!" she screamed at the feel of his limp penis. "Not again!" she cried in disgust, sending Marcus into a rage.

"Fuck you mean, 'not again'?" he growled.

"Nothing, baby," Tiffany said, trying to soothe him by

kissing his neck. But that only made matters worse, as the sweaty taste caused her to wretch.

"Sorry-ass bitch can't even get a nigga dick hard," he berated. He climbed up her body and pushed his penis in her face. "Open your mouth," he demanded, trying to force his way inside.

"Mmm…mmm," Tiffany mumbled, shaking her head furiously. The smell of his crotch overwhelmed her, causing her to gag.

Marcus took advantage of that and pushed himself inside of her mouth. Tiffany was in shock as he began humping her face. As soon as he got an erection, he rushed down to put it inside of her, but it was limp again by the time he got there. "Sorry-ass bitch!" Marcus said, climbing off of her. "'Bout to take me a shit," he announced, grabbing his pipe and a rock.

Tiffany had been in shock, but she sprang into action as soon as he left the room. She quickly dressed and grabbed her keys. She spied the pile of crack on the table and debated as to whether or not to take some. The debate lasted two seconds, and then the question became, *How much*? Her hand answered that question by sweeping it all into her purse. "Fuck you, too, bastard," she whispered, easing out the door.

"Say, bitch?" Marcus yelled, thinking he'd heard the door. When he didn't get a reply, he pinched off the turd he was working on and ran out into the room. His eyes first shot to where his drugs were and then darted around the rest of the room. Marcus snatched the door open just as Tiffany opened her car door. "My dope!" he yelled in horror as he took off in pursuit.

Tiffany laughed at the sight of the naked junkie as she pulled out of the parking lot. "Goodbye…and good riddance," she mused as she moved on to the next chapter of her life.

CHAPTER 9

Marcus was in a foul mood as he sat behind the wheel of the stolen car he and Pony were using for the day. It was just setting in that Tiffany was really gone. It had been almost a month since she had run out on him at the hotel and—as he put it—stolen his drugs. She'd refused his repeated calls for a week before changing her number. He realized he had gone too far that last time, disrespected her one too many times. "Damn!" Marcus yelled in disgust, pounding his fist against the wheel.

Pony was initially startled by the outburst, but he knew what was eating his friend. "You gotta let that shit go, shawty. She gone," he offered, genuinely concerned.

Marcus wanted to lash out at him and tell him to stay the fuck out of his business, but he knew Pony was right. He decided to take his wrath out on Alonzo instead. "Come on, ol' duck-ass nigga!" he yelled while laying on the car horn.

Alonzo, or "Big Zo" as he was referred to, was another junkie Marcus and Pony had recruited to pull their little capers. They were so hot in all the stores that it was impossible to even shop anywhere on the East Side of I-20. Being the masters of strategy that they were, they devised a new plan. Knowing that all eyes would be on them as soon as they walked in, Alonzo would be free to tear them a new one.

"We need to hit us a real lick," Marcus suggested, fingering the small pistol in his lap.

"I already told you like nine times that I ain't with that shit," Pony replied emphatically.

Lately, Marcus had been stressing committing an armed robbery, something Pony wanted no part of. Marcus was becoming more aggressive by the day. He'd been pulling his pistol on people at the slightest provocation. He was dying to get his gun off, and it was only a matter of time before he shot someone.

"You know that fat bastard ain't gon' let us cop nothing under a half," Marcus fumed.

Lately, P.I.G. had refused him entry unless he spent $500 or better, figuring he had set the bar high enough to keep the garbage out. Since Tiffany was coming by herself almost daily, Marcus served him no purpose. It was only out of loyalty to his uncle that he wasn't barred flat out.

"I know, shawty, but for one, P.I.G. got that glass. Ain't shit out here touching it. Two, if we get a half, we can get high and get our money back," Pony reasoned.

"Man, it's gonna take all day tryina boost $500," Marcus complained.

"If we a little short, maybe P.I.G. will let you sweep up." Pony chuckled.

Marcus shot him a dangerous glance, but the thought was too funny to get mad. "Nigga, you gon' be the one sweeping up," he said, cracking up.

At long last, Big Zo emerged from his house, dressed to steal. He sported a baggy pair of chinos that could hold a good amount of loot. The button-down shirt would allow him to easily stuff merchandise in there as well. A tie and glasses completed the look.

"Fuck took you so long?" Marcus demanded to know as Alonzo slid into the back seat.

"Say, how much Red pay for DVDs?" Big Zo asked Pony, totally ignoring Marcus.

Marcus fought the urge to turn around and shoot him in the head for trying him. Instead, he put the car in drive and pulled off.

"Shit, we can't get but five bucks a pop. We tryina strike bigger than that," Pony replied.

"We need more than a hundred DVDs your way," Marcus spat. "I'm tryina hit a real lick and rob me a nigga."

"I'm down for whatever, my nigga," Big Zo said enthusiastically.

"Well, I ain't down," Pony said forcefully, having grown tired of hearing about it.

"Scared! Say you scared, nigga," Big Zo chuckled from the rear.

"Scared…buy a dog or call the cops," Marcus laughed, now glad he hadn't shot Alonzo.

* * *

Big Zo waited several minutes after Marcus and Pony walked into Walmart before making his own entrance.

As predicted, security immediately flocked to the known thieves. They could have easily made them leave, but they wanted to catch them in the act and have them locked up. Plainclothes agents trailed the men as the security cameras followed them from above. To amuse themselves, Marcus and Pony abruptly split up. The surveillance split up as well, trailing the men.

With all the security busy, Big Zo made a beeline to the Electronics Department. He began loading his bag with the newest releases. He couldn't believe his eyes or his luck when a careless clerk walked away from an open display case filled with expensive electronics. "Shut my mouth," Alonzo mumbled as he moved on the merchandise. He grabbed ten of the most expensive digital cameras and put them in the bag. A good thief knows when to quit, and Big Zo was a good thief. He fought the urge to grab more and walked away just as the salesclerk returned.

On the way out, Big Zo gave Marcus a slight nod, indicating that the deed was done. On cue, Marcus took off running, with security in pursuit. The commotion signaled Pony to do the same. The agents following him were sure he hadn't lifted anything, but he was running so they chased him anyway.

All hell broke loose as the guards chased the crackheads through the aisles. They were both tackled near the exit as Alonzo calmly walked out with his stash.

The silly crackheads giggled hysterically as the guards searched them.

"We got you red-handed," an overzealous, overweight guard wheezed as their pockets were searched.

"You got shit!" Pony laughed as the frisk came up empty.

They were warned, photographed, threatened, and told not to ender the store ever again.

Alonzo, a junkie through and through, fought the urge to run off with his plunder, ultimately deciding against it. He knew he would eventually cross them, but it wasn't going to be today. He ducked down in the back seat of the car to prevent being seen with the known thief. The guard followed Marcus and Pony to the stolen car and wrote down the plate number.

"You can get up now, ol' hide-and-seek-ass nigga," Marcus laughed as he pulled onto Panola Road.

"What'd ya get?" Pony inquired anxiously.

"A little something-something," he bragged, producing one of the cameras.

"Damn! These shit's nice," Pony exclaimed.

Marcus swerved the car, trying to get a look for himself.

"Three dollars a pop," Big Zo said proudly, "and I got ten of dem, guys."

"Red cheap ass ain't gon' give us but a buck a piece," Marcus complained.

"Shit, that put us where we need to be," Pony said.

Alonzo decided his co-conspirators didn't need to know about the DVDs and assorted knickknacks stuffed in his clothes. *A little something for a rainy day*, he thought to himself.

* * *

Most of the older homes on Red's street had been bought, razed, and replaced with McManions built in their place. He was one of the few holdouts when the developers came through offering peanuts. As a result, the small home he paid $30,000 for twenty years ago was now worth a small fortune.

Red had cake already. He was one of the major fences in the city. He bought and sold anything that could be bought or sold. His house was a virtual warehouse of goods. The walls were lined with flat-screen TVs all hooked up to showcase picture quality. There were several complete living room suites for sale as well. The kitchen was stocked with every appliance and gadget known to man. "From Picasso to pussy" was Red's mantra, and he had it all for sale. The police knew who and what he was, but they only came through to shop or to be paid off.

Red was well into his fifties, but he dressed in the latest fashions that kids wore. His salt-and-pepper hair was kept freshly braided by one of the young girls he kept around the house. He wasn't just a sugar daddy; he was a baby daddy knocking young girls up on the regular. Besides the ten grown sons he had with his first wife, he had another forty or fifty kids on the side. Two of his current girlfriends were pregnant now, neither of them even twenty years old.

Red greeted the trio of Marcus, Pony, and Big Zo warmly as he let them in. He had no security to speak of; if a person knew him, he knew them, and that was good enough. Besides, he had ten grown sons and nephews who were well-known goons. Anybody would be a fool to try and rob Red. "Let me see what ya got," he asked the men eagerly.

"We came up on some cameras," Marcus, the unofficial spokesman, said, handing one to Red for inspection.

"Dese nice rat here," Red announced, showcasing his third-grade education.

As he checked out the cameras, Marcus scanned the room with larceny in his eyes.

Pony read his mind and gave him a terse headshake when their eyes met. He knew a man would have to be a fool to try Red, and Marcus was a fool.

"My neighbors gon' love dese," Red said, referring to the young white professionals who now inhabited his street. His law-abiding neighbors loved a good deal, stolen goods or not—"hot shit for a cool price," as one put it. "How many you got? I'll take 'em all," Red announced, looking to corner the stolen camera market.

"We got ten. Give us a stack," Big Zo blurted, out of turn.

"A stack, huh?" Red pondered, even though he was prepared to go to $1,200. "A'ight," he sad reluctantly. "For y'all, I'll do a grand."

Marcus gasped audibly when Red produced a huge wad of cash and began peeling hundreds off of it. Pony saw a deadly glint in his friend's eye as he watched him count the money.

Just as Red was handing over the cash, the front door swung open. "Hey, Daddy," two of Red's sons said in unison, heading to the rear of the house. They returned immediately with guns in both hands.

"We 'bout to take dese to mark dem," one son said, holding up one of the H&K MP5 submachine guns.

"A'ight. Y'all be careful now," Red warned as they left.

Pony gave Marcus a raised brow look that said, *"See?"* Marcus nodded in agreement, knowing he'd have to find an easier lick.

"If y'all got some mo' of dese, holla," Red said as he escorted the men to the door. "Laptops too!" he added.

"That's what's up," Pony said over his shoulder as they exited the house.

* * *

"Man, I was 'bout to get dat nigga," Marcus proclaimed once they were back in the car.

"Nigga, you was about to get us kilt," Pony corrected.

"Man, what y'all talking about?" Big Zo asked, having

missed the unspoken exchange back in the house.

"This crazy fool wanna rob Red," Pony said.

"Now that's what's up! Did you see that bankroll?" Big Zo exclaimed.

"This nigga scared though," Marcus said, hooking his thumb over at Pony beside him.

"Whatever, but I ain't robbin' Red or nobody else," Pony spat back emphatically.

* * *

A freak show was going full blast when the trio arrived at P.I.G.'s. As they walked in, their attention immediately went to the action on the floor, where two men were vigorously humping each end of a well-built young woman. She had large breasts that complemented her hard stomach and her round ass. Her shoulder-length hair was in disarray from the pounding she was taking. When their gaze finally made it to her face, they could see something was off about the girl, who was in her late teens at best. She had the slanted eyes of someone impaired with Down's Syndrome, and she appeared oblivious to what the men were doing to her. Even when the man in front pulled out of her mouth and ejaculated in her face, she barely blinked. The blank expression she wore on her face didn't change, no matter what they did.

"Y'all want some of this?" P.I.G. asked jovially when he noticed Marcus and company.

"Naw, we cool," Marcus said, wishing he had time for a quick romp. But he hadn't had a blast all day, and it was first things first.

"You sure? She do anything! She retarded, and I just bought her," he added.

"Just let us get an onion so we can push," Pony said bluntly. He was sickened at the sight of the helpless girl being abused.

Earl was taken aback by the tone but understood. He knew his boss was a sick dude, but this was a new low—even for The Notorious P.I.G. "Gimme a stack. I'll hook it up," Earl said, feeling him.

Pony had to get Marcus's attention to get the money.

Marcus handed it over and focused back on the action.

Earl was back in a flash with the dope. "I threw you an extra eight ball," he whispered as he handed the package to Pony. Earl made sure to stress the point that the hookup was on the strength of him.

"Y'all staying here?" Pony asked curtly as he exited the open door.

Marcus and Alonzo pried themselves away from the show and followed him out.

"That's who the fuck we need to rob," Pony fumed once they were back in the car.

"No you're talking!" Marcus exclaimed. "That's what's up."

CHAPTER 10

Tiffany paced her small room like a tiger in a cage, deep in thought and pondering where her next hit was coming from. "I don't know what the fuck I was thinking." She cursed herself. In a brief moment of clarity, she'd convinced herself to pay her bills on payday instead of buying dope. Now she didn't have a dime to spend on getting high. The full tank of gas and paid receipts were no consolation. She wanted to get high.

Her days of snorting were behind her once she smoked that first primo at the hotel. She'd chipped away at the few grams she'd taken from Marcus until they were depleted entirely. She loved the intense high that smoking gave her. A few sizzling pulls from a blunt, and she was zone coasting. Snorting just couldn't compare to that. Tiffany had vowed to stop getting high every day, but it was a vow she broke every day.

Payday was days away, so she was faced with the dilemma of how to raise some capital. "Yeah, right." She chuckled as the notion to hit her parents up for cash crossed her mind. She knew she'd milked that cow dry. Her father had forbidden her mother from giving her another dime.

Inspiration struck when she spied Carlos in his driveway across the street. Figuring he'd be good for a loan that would never be paid back, she sprang into action.

Tiffany was halfway down the stairs when she took stock of the huge sweatpants and T-shirt she had on. She decided she'd change close and help her cause. Back in her room, she swapped her sweats for a pair of Daisy Dukes. She removed her bra and tied a knot in her shirt to expose her hard stomach.

Carlos was just finishing up washing his car when Tiffany came out of her house. Even from across the street, she could see his eyes lock on her breasts that bounced freely as she hopped down her front steps. Tiffany was amused by the shocked expression Carlos wore as she made her way over to him. Then came her turn to be shocked.

Carlos's front door opened, and a stunning young lady gracefully exited. "Hey, baby. You done?" she asked sweetly. Her beauty made the question sound like a love song.

Tiffany's heart stopped as the girl made her way over and kissed Carlos on his lips. She was in awe of how pretty the female was. The woman was almost white with long, almost blonde hair and green eyes. The tasteful summer dress could not conceal the voluptuous figure underneath it. The girl was a knockout, plain and simple.

"Oh, who's your little friend?" she asked, scanning Tiffany with her eyes.

Tiffany crossed her arms in an effort to conceal herself, now embarrassed by her hoochie mama getup.

"Huh? Oh, this is my lil sister," Carlos said, regaining his bearings.

"Hey, lil sis," the woman sang genially.

"Yeah…um, hey," Tiffany said, wishing she could pull a *Bewitched* and wiggle her nose and disappear. Instead, she turned quickly on her heels and headed home.

"Hey, Tiff!" Carlos called from her rear. "Did you need something?"

Tiffany could only shake her head. No way was she gonna let them see the tears falling freely from her eyes.

* * *

The crushing disappointment only fueled Tiffany's desire to get high. With no other options, she gathered up some of her jewelry from her dresser. She decided she could live without all the trinkets Marcus had given her over the years. She threw in a few of her own pieces to augment the slum jewelry Marcus was able to afford.

In her haste, she almost left wearing her costume. "Uh-uh!" She chuckled when she caught a glimpse of her scantily clad self in the mirror. She purposely selected a summer dress similar to the one worn by Carlos's girlfriend and set out.

Since all the pawnshops were pretty much the same in her estimate, Tiffany finally selected one based on nothing more than its pretty sign. Once inside, she waited impatiently as the lone clerk helped a customer. The delay proved to be instructive, as she was able to learn the pawning process. She learned that she could reclaim her property by a certain time. She lied to herself, vowing that she would return on payday to get her jewelry back.

"Yes?" the unprofessional clerk inquired curtly.

"I need some money for these," Tiffany replied, carefully

laying out her jewelry for inspection.

"How much you tryina get?" he asked, looking the pieces over.

"I guess about $500 should do it," Tiffany said naively.

The clerk looked stunned for a second and then began to laugh. *Surely she must be joking*, he thought, but he soon realized she wasn't because of the serious look on her face. "Can't give you that much," he offered contritely.

"How much then?" Tiffany asked, the sting of being laughed at evident in her voice.

"I can go $100," the clerk replied in a take-it-or-leave-it tone.

She was insulted, but no so much as to turn down the offer. After a few forms, fingerprints, and a photograph, she was on her way…on her way to P.I.G.'s place.

* * *

After P.I.G. hung up from Tiffany informing him that she was on her way, he cleared some of the stragglers from the room. He was delighted to see her again.

Blast eyed him suspiciously, curious as to his sudden change of demeanor.

"Earl, when Tiffany gets here, I want you to stall before serving her," P.I.G. said, giddy about his plan.

Blast sucked her teeth and stormed off at the mention of the girl's name.

Tiffany had never seen P.I.G.'s house so empty. Besides P.I.G. and Earl, there was only the young girl coloring in her coloring book on the floor. She was confused as to why the obviously retarded girl was there and why she was dressed in a negligee that was clearly not age appropriate. "Can I have an eight ball please?" Tiffany asked politely, extending the cash to Earl.

"Sure, but it's gonna be a second. We still bagging up," Earl said, retreating to the rear.

"Have a seat," P.I.G. said sweetly. "Where is your lil man?"

"Oh, we not together anymore," she replied, confirming what he had heard.

"That's good to hear." P.I.G. smiled, attempting to be sexy. "Gina!" he called loudly to break her from the trance of the coloring books.

When the girl looked up with her crooked stare, P.I.G. leaned back and pulled out an enormous penis. Tiffany did a double-take, not believing her eyes. An even bigger shock came when Gina knelt in front of him and took as much of him in her mouth as she could. Tiffany watched in horror as the handicapped girl feverishly worked her head up and down. She was relieved when Blast came out and tossed a package on the table; Tiffany just wanted to get out of there.

P.I.G. held his tongue at the deliberate attempt at sabotaging his plan.

"Um, excuse me, Blast," Tiffany said after looking at the drugs. "If you don't mind, I wanted it hard," she asked sheepishly.

The realization that Tiffany was now smoking crack was too much for P.I.G. He knew her decline would have to come at some point. As he looked at her, imagining himself in her mouth, he exploded in Gina's.

The force almost knocked the girl over, but Gina just sat there as P.I.G. emptied his scrotum in her face.

"Go clean up," Blast ordered as she came back with the dope. She tossed the package to Tiffany and then said, "Take it with you."

Tiffany looked at P.I.G. for approval to leave with the drugs. "Is it okay?" she inquired, using her baby girl voice that worked so well on her daddy.

The phony display caused Blast to suck her teeth again as she helped clean Gina off.

"Yeah, go on, sweetie," he replied, still stroking his huge penis.

Wanda was just pulling up as Tiffany made it to the curb. "Hey, girl!" Wanda sang cheerfully, as if they were the closest of friends.

"Hey yaself!" Tiffany replied, matching her tone.

"Ima 'bout to grab something. Wait for me, and we'll hang out," Wanda offered.

"That's cool," she said, intending to smoke Wanda's dope. When Wanda disappeared into P.I.G.'s house, Tiffany quickly took out a gram to use with her and saved the rest for herself.

Minutes later, Wanda returned and led the way to her house.

* * *

When they arrived, Tiffany placed her paltry offering on the table. "It's on me today," Tiffany announced proudly. The small amount would last her a day or two, but that was one blunt for Wanda.

"P.I.G. sold you that?" she exclaimed.

"Yeah. He hooked me up cuz my money be short. He can be cool when he want to," Tiffany replied.

"The only thing cool about that fat bastard is the ice water running through his veins," she said.

"That nigga like me, so I showed him a little leg." Tiffany giggled.

It was at that moment that Wanda saw just how naïve her little friend really was. In that same moment, she decided she would use the girl for whatever she could squeeze out of her. "A'ight. You showed him a little leg, huh? That nigga gon' have you sweepin' up." She laughed.

"What is this 'sweeping up' I keep hearing about?" Tiffany asked curiously.

"Gurrrl…you do NOT want to know," Wanda said emphatically. "And what's up with that little retarded girl?"

"Girl…you…do…NOT…want…to…know!" Tiffany said, repulsed by the memory.

Tiffany was taken aback when during small talk, Wanda put the entire amount of crack into the blunt. As she rolled, Tiffany filled her in on Blast's behavior.

"I can't believe she think someone wants her man," Wanda said, lighting the blunt. The drug sizzled loudly as she inhaled deeply.

Tiffany caught herself inhaling along with her as she had the blunt. When she did get the blunt for her turn, she pulled on it as if her life depended on it. The heavily laced blunt hit her instantly. A current-like wave swept over her as the powerful drug coursed through her system. The days of skimpy blunts were over. Tiffany was on to the next chapter.

CHAPTER 11

Tiffany shook her head when she saw Kim walking in the store. "She look a hot mess." She chuckled to herself.

Even with her hair done and some of Tiffany's church clothes, she still looked like a junkie. Since the sting was working, it really didn't matter. For the last two weeks, the women's plan had been successful. Tiffany was using legitimate customers' credit cards for Kim to make purchases. Kim would simply then return the merchandise for a cash refund.

It took a week for the store auditors to become aware of the irregularity, and it took security another day to identify the culprits.

Five separate sets of eyes followed Kim through the store as she gathered high-ticket items. Two new undercover guards discreetly tailed her, while Mrs. Lovejoy and two others watched the monitors in her office.

Kim, meanwhile, was having trouble staying focused on the business at hand due to the small piece of cocaine in her purse, demanding to be smoked. "Okay, okay! Ima smoke you. Dang!" Kim said to the drug as she detoured to the nearest restroom.

"What the hell is this crazy bitch doing?" Tiffany said when Kim turned off. "I know she ain't 'bout to take no blast up in here," she said, recognizing that look in her eyes. She was now very familiar with that look; it was one she often saw in her own eyes. She understood the yearning, when that old Rob Base song played in the head, "I Wanna Rock Right Now," and that monkey on your back goes to squealing. She knew there was no stopping it. "Shit, I could use a little pick-me-up my damn self," Tiffany admitted.

It was a good thing the restroom was empty, not that it mattered to Kim. She rushed into the first stall and went to work. Kim whipped out her shooter from one shoe and her lighter from the other. She fished out the small piece of crack from her purse as a guard peered over the wall from the next stall.

The guard almost blew her composure and surveillance when she realized what Kim was doing. She couldn't believe the little junkie had the audacity to smoke crack cocaine in the bathroom of a major department store in the middle of the day. The guard fought off the urge to strangle the little crack addict. She ducked back down and went outside to pick up her target once she left the restroom.

The guard had been brought in from another store, since it was an internal theft. She had been watching Tiffany for a couple of days and felt bad for her. It was clear that her parents invested a lot of time, energy, and love in her upbringing. She had no doubt that the girl had some nigga come along and undo what her parents did with his soft words and his hard dick. It would be a useful intervention, the guard reasoned, remembering how she had strayed herself. Luckily, the people in her own life stuck by her and got her through it.

"What the fuck took you so long?" Tiffany barked through clenched teeth when Kim finally made it to her register.

"I had to pee," Kim lied, her mouth twitching uncontrollably. "Mmmhmm," Tiffany replied, ringing up the clothing. This, their second lick of the day, came to over $900. They had struck $400 just a few hours earlier.

With them becoming more brazen and more frequent, Mrs. Lovejoy decided it was the day to make her move.

Tiffany she was getting careless, but she had to have it. Every since she had smoked that heavily laced blunt with Wanda, her usage had doubled. She was blazing her way through an eight ball of hard every day now, but even that was a pittance compared to what Kim ran through her shooter every day.

"Thank you. Come again," Tiffany said professionally as she handed Kim her purchase.

"Oh, I will." Kim giggled, amused by their scheme.

Tiffany's expression changed to horror when she saw security approaching.

Kim saw it and turned to investigate. "Oh shit!" Kim exclaimed and tried to run for it. Being a crack whore, she was pretty nimble, a skill honed from darting through the traffic in pursuit of johns. She made it exactly two steps before being apprehended by the large female guard.

"You two come along quietly," Mrs. Lovejoy said sternly. "No need to embarrass yourselves any further."

"Wh-what's going on?" Tiffany stammered most unconvincingly.

"We'll discuss it in my office," Mrs. Lovejoy said, leading the way.

The group followed in silence as Tiffany's co-workers

pointed and whispered.

"Sit down," Mrs. Lovejoy demanded as she sat behind her desk. "Not you!" she said to Kim, who tried to take the empty seat next to Tiffany. "You stand!" She looked at Tiffany, with a hurt expression on her face. "I cannot believe you have been stealing," the supervisor said, her voice on the edge of breaking. "I've known you your whole life. I remember when you were born," she continued as a single tear escaped her eye.

Tiffany was unmoved by the display of emotion. All she was concerned with was how she was gonna get high. A slight smile spread across her lips when she remembered the $200 in her car from the earlier lick.

"Do you find this amusing?" Mrs. Lovejoy demanded, misunderstanding the smirk.

Tiffany remained mute, her eyes glued to the floor in front of her.

"Well? What have you got to say for yourself?" Mrs. Lovejoy asked, pounding her desk. "What's gotten into you?"

"Excuse me, ma'am," the plainclothes guard interjected. "I believe I can answer that." She snatched Kim's shoe off and held up the crack pipe.

As ominous as it looked, Mrs. Lovejoy had no idea what it was.

"It's a pipe to smoke crack cocaine," the guard explained, answering the tacit question contorting the supervisor's face. "This one was smoking drugs in our bathroom," she added, thrusting a finger at Kim.

Mrs. Lovejoy gasped. "Tiffany, tell me you are NOT using drugs!"

"No. I—" was all Tiffany could get out before another

guard spoke up.

"Ma'am, she is definitely using drugs," she said solemnly. "I know the signs. My sister just passed from drug use."

"This is going to absolutely kill your mother," Mrs. Lovejoy announced.

"Please!" Tiffany begged. "Please don't tell my mama." She clasped her hands as if in prayer as she begged for respite. "Please! I'll pay back every penny," she pleaded.

"I'm sorry, but it is out of my hands now," came the supervisor's reply. She nodded her head to the guard at the door.

On cue, the guard opened the door, and in walked two Dekalb County police officers.

Tiffany had never experienced the feel of handcuffs before, but it was business as usual for Kim. The women were marched right through the store as everyone looked on.

"I am so dead," Tiffany cried in anguish as the full reality came to her. "My mama's gonna die, but she's gonna kill me first."

Kim, on the other hand, was unfazed. "Girl, you fine," she said, trying to console her young friend. "Ain't nothing but a Class C felony. You gonna get to sign your own bond and be home by supper," Kim advised as the grim reality of her own situation became clear. Kim had violated her probation months earlier and had an arrest warrant waiting on her. That crack pipe in her shoe ensured that she wouldn't be getting a bond. The best she could hope for was a lengthy stay in rehab. Of course, there was an eighteen-month wait just to get into the program. "That's what I get for trying some new shit," Kim whined. "Shoulda stuck to sucking dicks."

* * *

The police cruiser pulled out of the crowded mall parking lot and onto Candler Road. It merged onto 20 East, then 285 toward Memorial Drive.

As soon as the massive jail came into view, both women began crying, albeit for different reasons. Tiffany had seen the structure almost every day of her life, but never in her wildest dreams would she have thought she'd be taken there in handcuffs.

Once inside, the women were photographed, fingerprinted, and given a cursory medical exam as part of the intake process.

They were given the opportunity to use a phone after they were booked in. Kim declined, having long ago burned all of her bridges, leaving no one to call.

Tiffany, however, jumped at the chance when her turn came. She quickly dialed most of the numbers to her house before changing her mind. "I know!" she said, dialing most of Carlos's number before hanging up again. "Think, girl…" Then she smiled as it came to her. She dialed the numbers she'd only recently committed to memory. Tiffany was delighted when her new friend picked up on the second ring.

"Dekalb County Jail? What'd you do now, Mike?" Wanda exclaimed, assuming it was her boyfriend, who was no stranger to trouble himself.

"It's me, Tiffany. I need some help," Tiffany pleaded in her baby girl voice. She then gave Wanda a brief synopsis of her situation.

Wanda admonished her about the stupidity of her plan and, using a crackhead to pull it off. "Girl, I'm on the way," she said when she heard a deputy tell Tiffany her time was up.

Both women, along with a few other recent arrestees, were taken across the street to see a judge. Like Kim told her, Tiffany was allowed to sign her own bond, but Kim herself was stuck. Tiffany was given a court date and a warning of the dire consequences if she missed it. Back a the jail, she was out-processed and released.

* * *

"Thank you so much," Tiffany cried, hugging Wanda tightly in the jail waiting room.

"No problem, lil mama," Wanda replied, pressing her body against Tiffany's.

Once they got in Wanda's new Lexus, she handed Tiffany a tightly rolled Swisher Sweet blunt. "I know you need this, girl."

Tiffany stopped short of lighting it, remembering she had to go face her parents.

"Go on and keep it," Wanda offered after Tiffany explained her dilemma. "Shit, you need to bring yo' lil fine ass down to the club and get some of this money. You get cash every day and won't have to worry 'bout how you gon' get high," Wanda said as she drove. "Sure beats pulling capers with a junkie."

Tiffany was too dark for Wanda to see her blushing at the "fine" compliment. She thought of herself as marginally cute at best, but never fine. To Tiffany, Wanda was fine, like a brown-skinned version of *Beyoncé.* "Girl, I may just hafta do dat," Tiffany replied in sista girl mode. She knew she could never and would never take her clothes off in front of strange men, not even for money.

"May as well. Lawd know you ain't got no job no more," Wanda said, pulling next to Tiffany's car in the mall lot.

"Thanks again," Tiffany said, leaning in to give Wanda another hug.

Wanda sneaked her with a kiss on her lips before embracing her. "No problem, girl. Call me later and let me know how you make out," she said.

"Okay, I will," Tiffany replied, pulling out of the awkward embrace.

"Let me know if you wanna come down to the club," Wanda called out as Tiffany got into her car.

"I will," Tiffany lied, knowing full well she wasn't. "Ima call."

* * *

The usually short drive home seemed to take only a few seconds. Tiffany still hadn't come up with a plausible explanation of the day's events. Unable to come up with anything, she decided to wing it when she got there.

Tiffany was dismayed to see that her parents were waiting for her in the front room. It was a room rarely used, if ever, but it prevented her from slipping past. "Hey, Mama, Daddy," she said meekly to her grim-faced parents.

"Have a seat, young lady," her father said stoically.

Tiffany looked to her mother for support but got none; she averted her eyes.

"Well, Mrs. Lovejoy called us," her father said, his statement sounding more like a question.

Oddly, Tiffany felt more irritation than fear. She hadn't had a blast since early that morning, and father or not, the dude was questioning her.

"Well?" he asked, frustrated by her silence. "You wanna tell us what happened?"

"Calm down, Will," Tiffany's mom said, patting her husband's leg.

"It's all a big misunderstanding," Tiffany began, figuring she'd adlib as she went along.

"That's what I thought," her mom chimed in, eager for the whole sordid mess to be easy to explain away. "It was that girl, wasn't it? The one with the drugs?"

"Uh huh. It was, Mama. It was that girl!" Tiffany said excitedly, happy her mother had come through with an excuse.

Her father sighed loudly as his wife began doing exactly what she had promised not to do. "Tiffany, go up to your room so your mother and I can talk for a minute," he said, exasperated.

"Okay, Daddy," she replied, rising to her feet. Before leaving the room, Tiffany ran over and hugged her mother's neck. "I'm sorry, Mama," she said, cementing her support.

Tiffany's parents began debating as to how to deal with the situation, even before she got out of the room.

She hit the stairs two at a time to make the most of the time she had. *Surely I got time for a quick blast.* She was long overdue and definitely deserved one after all she'd been through that day. She started to open the window and hang her head out like she used to do when she was just smoking weed. Then she remembered how the smoke would still come in, and she quickly abandoned the idea. Tiffany then decided she would just smoke in her bathroom, using the steam from the shower to mask the odor. In her haste, she forgot to lock her bedroom or bathroom door. She smiled, pleased with her cleverness as she turned on the vent and climbed on the toilet to blow the smoke in. One pull told her Wanda had packed the blunt to the gills. It sizzled loudly with each hearty pull she took. With each pull, Tiffany agreed to out the blunt, but every pull led to another. She was so caught up listening to the crack crackle that she didn't hear her parents enter her room.

Her father finally got her mother to agree not to stick up for her and force her to explain herself.

"She's in the shower. Poor thing's had a rough day. We should wait till morning, Will," Tiffany's mother whispered.

"Mary, please!" her father shot back, irritated at the attempt to let the girl off the hook again.

"Okay, okay!" she agreed. "I'll stick my head in and tell her to come to our room when she gets out." She neared the bathroom. "Oh my!" Tiffany's mother gasped, stumbling away from the door.

"What?" her father asked, rushing to investigate.

She was too astonished to speak, just pointing to the bathroom door.

Will pushed the door open, expecting the worst—and that was exactly what he got.

Tiffany was perched precariously atop the toilet, feverishly sucking on the cigar. She choked harshly when she finally saw her shocked parents. "Don't you people fucking knock!?" she screamed between coughs.

"Is that marijuana?" her naïve mother asked.

"That's freebase!" her father exclaimed, using the terminology of his era.

"Freebase?" Mary asked, still confused. "You mean… like Richard Pryor?"

"Richard Pryor, Bobby, and Whitney, O.D.B.!" Tiffany screamed, furious at the interruption. She took another pull as she climbed down, then outed the blunt on her sink.

Both of her parents were in absolute shock, speechless, staring at the stranger wearing their child's body.

"Fuck wrong with y'all?" Tiffany asked nonchalantly. "No big thang. I get high erry now and then."

"Not in MY house you won't!" her father boomed indignantly.

"YOUR house?" Tiffany chuckled. "Nigga, dis OUR house."

"Tiffany!" her mother screamed. "What has gotten into you!? Apologize this instant!"

"What?" Tiffany yelled back. "Apologize for what? This nigga don't run shit 'round here."

Her father rushed over and grabbed Tiffany by both shoulders, desperately searching her face for his daughter.

"Get the fuck off me, nigga," she spat, pulling out of his grasp.

Before he could stop it, his open palm shot up and collided with the side of her face. The sound of the slap seemed to stop time as it reverberated in the room.

They all stood for several seconds in total silence until Tiffany finally spoke up. "You ever touch me again, muhfucka, Ima kill you," Tiffany spat with an evil smirk.

Her father moved forward to see if she could keep her word, but he was stopped by his wife.

"No, Will. Please!" she begged as she struggled to restrain the man.

"Hold up, Mary. I'm tryina see what she talking about," he replied, trying to get around her.

"Let him go!" Tiffany challenged. "Come on, nigga."

"I want you out my house now," her father said calmly.

"You ain't saying nothing," Tiffany taunted.

"If you ain't gone in twenty minutes, Ima toss your little ass out on your head," he replied before turning on his heels and leaving the room.

Mary turned her head back and forth from her husband to her daughter, desperately torn as to who to defend. "Don't you move," she demanded as firmly as she could before rushing out to her husband.

As soon as her mother left the room, Tiffany began stuffing clothes in her bag. She gathered as much as she could with one hand, the precious blunt still tightly clutched in the other.

Mary got nowhere with her husband and returned to talk some sense into her daughter. But when she got back to Tiffany's room, she found it empty.

* * *

Once inside her car, Tiffany debated what to do and where to go. Carlos was the first person she thought to seek refuge with, but his girlfriend's car in the driveway killed that idea.

Her phone vibrated in her purse as she slowly pulled down her street. A quick check of the caller ID made up her mind as to her destination. "Hey, Wanda," Tiffany answered, sounding as pitiful as she could.

"Girl, you okay?" Wanda asked, as if she was really concerned. "I was calling to see how you made out with your mama and daddy."

"They put me out. I don't know where Ima go," Tiffany replied, already heading toward Wanda's house.

"Come on over here, girl. You know I got yo' back," Wanda offered.

"You sure?" Tiffany asked rhetorically.

"Yeah, girl, come on. Ima have one rolled up when you

get here," Wanda said.

It was then that Tiffany realized she was still clutching the blunt in her head with a death grip. Not intending to share it, she tucked it away in the glove box for safekeeping.

* * *

The guest room in Wanda's house was roughly the same size as the one Tiffany left behind. It contained a brass daybed, a small dresser, and its own bathroom. Tiffany set her bags down and went to join Wanda in the front room.

"Girl, you just in time," Wanda exclaimed, holding up a tightly rolled blunt.

Tiffany watched in awe as Wanda lit it and inhaled deeply. Again, Tiffany inhaled with her.

"You…o…kay…gurl?" Wanda inquired in between gulps of air.

"No," Tiffany whined. "I'm a mess—homeless, jobless, broke. I don't know what Ima do."

"You know you can come down to da club," Wanda said, passing the blunt.

"I ain't ready for that," Tiffany admitted before hitting the blunt with gusto.

Wanda peeped the greedy pull and knew the girl would soon be open for anything. That, of course, would be to her benefit, and a plan crept into her mind. "I got your back. You can stay here as long as you need to, but you'll need some income. Yer gon' have to help out," she announced.

"I guess I hafta find another job," Tiffany sighed.

"A job!?" Wanda exclaimed with a chuckle. "Girl, a job ain't nothing but work, and I can't be waiting on you to get no check."

"What else can I do? I can't dance," Tiffany said in the same whiney tone that was beginning to annoy Wanda.

Wanda knew she had her hook, line, and sinker, but she was moving too fast. She decided to pull back a little and turn her out slowly. "I'll tell you what…" Wanda began in a more sympathetic tone. "Mike is coming over in a little while. Ima see if he got anything else you can do." She knew just getting the young girl inside the club was half the battle. *This is the other half,* Wanda mused to herself as she passed the cocaine-filled blunt.

"As long as I can keep my clothes on. I aint' no ho," Tiffany said before taking a big pull.

Wanda flinched slightly at the insult but said nothing. She knew full well that she was a ho and much worse, but she didn't like being called one. "Gurrl, if you did dance, you would make a killin'! You way finer than most dem chicks at the club," Wanda said matter-of-factly.

"Yeah, right." Tiffany giggled, blushing unseen under her dark skin.

"Fo' real, gurl. Dem hoes got bullet holes and stab wounds," Wanda joked.

In fact, Club Chocolate had the baddest dancers in the ATL, most of them turned out by Wanda herself. All of them had been personally sampled by Mike—some even by Wanda.

"Come on. Lemme see what ya got," Wanda said, hitting a button on the remote control. "Whose Pussy" by rapper D-lite boomed through the Bose speakers as Wanda rose to her feet. "Come on! I'm finna show you some moves," she told a giggling Tiffany, pulling her up by the hands.

Tiffany was high as a barrel of oil and got into the vibe. She began dancing all the latest dances as Wanda watched.

"Hold up," Wanda announced and bolted from the room.

Tiffany was feeling the song's heavy bass line and kept on dancing.

Wanda returned in a flash with a large tote bag in hand. "Come on and find something in your size," she said, dumping out an assortment of lingerie.

Tiffany hesitated for a second until she saw that the undergarments were new, with the tags still attached. "This is nice," she said, holding up a bra and thong set.

"Go on and put it on," Wanda said, beginning to shed her own clothes to put on the set she selected.

Tiffany watched in awe as Wanda came out of her clothes. More fascination than lust had Tiffany stuck in her place.

Wanda caught it but didn't react. She'd hoped to get to sex the girl herself, but she wasn't sure if Tiffany would be up for it.

Tiffany finally caught herself and went to her room to change. She admired herself in the mirror for a second before going back out. "Well?" she asked, holding her arms out for inspection.

"Lemme see. Turn around," Wanda said, coming closer. "Oh, this is nice," she said, fondling Tiffany's breast under the guise of adjusting her bra.

Tiffany blushed again as she soaked the thong from Wanda's touch. *I...am...not...gay*, she told herself firmly, confused by her reaction to the woman's touch.

Wanda caught the reaction and pulled back. *Be easy*, she warned herself, feeling moisture seeping into her boy shorts. "Lemme show you a few moves," Wanda said, hitting the replay button on the CD player. She ran Tiffany through a regiment of stripper moves. She showed her how to make her ass cheeks clap, shake it like a salt shaker, get down and get her eagle on, and an assortment of other seductive dances.

The women were so engrossed in their revelry that neither heard the door open behind them while they danced. Mike stood there watching in silence until Tiffany caught a glimpse of him. She announced his presence with a shriek and took off down the hall.

"Girl, that's Mike!" Wanda called behind her, laughing.

"Who dat?" Mike demanded, not bothering to hide his interest nor needing to.

"That's my little get-high partner," Wanda said, pressing her body against his.

"She dance?" he asked, still staring down the empty hall.

"Not yet, but gimme a sec. You know how I do," Wanda boasted.

"You know dem tricks love dem some young broads," Mike said, finally looking at Wanda.

"*Dem* niggas, huh?" Wanda teased, grabbing his manhood through his pants.

"Oh, Ima keep it 100 percent real. I wanna hit dat too," Mike admitted eagerly.

"Shit, me too, but we gotta go slow. Shawty green," Wanda said, still stroking him.

Tiffany returned a short time later, fully dressed and partially embarrassed.

Wanda made the introduction, giving Tiffany the opportunity to get a good look at Mike.

Mike stood a hair over six-two and had the solid build of an athlete. His smooth, bald head was an interesting contrast to the neatly trimmed full beard adorning his face. He looked, dressed, and smelled like money. To Tiffany, he resembled a darker version of Suge Knight, minus the gut.

"Wanda tells me you're looking for a job," Mike said,

staring into Tiffany's eyes—in fact, past her eyes and straight into her soul.

"Um, yeah, but I don't dance. We was just playing," she said, feeling the need to explain herself.

"That's fine. I got plenty of dancers. What I need is a good hostess," Mike offered.

"What I gotta do?" Tiffany asked cautiously, as she was unfamiliar with the term.

"Check ID, take admission fees. You may have to help serve erry now and then, but you get tips when you do," he explained. "It pays $200 a night," Mike said, sealing the deal.

"I'll take it!" Tiffany practically shouted at her good fortune. "When can I start?"

"I'll bring her tomorrow," Wanda interjected, cozying back up to Mike.

"Thank you so much, Mr. Mike. Ima leave you guys alone now," Tiffany said before retreating.

"Okay. Nice meeting you. See you tomorrow," Mike replied, watching her backside as she left. "Lil mama is a goldmine!" Mike exclaimed. "I can't wait to smash that."

"Well, until then, you need to come and smash this," Wanda said, placing his hand on her ass.

Tiffany instantly missed her showerhead as the sounds of lovemaking drifted through the thin walls. She lit what was left of the blunt she'd started at home as she listened. The couple stopped making love and began to straight-out fuck. Not only could she hear Wanda's moans and Mike's growls as he pounded in and out of her, but the rhythmic sound of the headboard slamming into the wall as their bodies collided. The sound of skin slapping together echoed in the silent room. She wasn't even aware that her hand slipped into her panties until she felt a tingle shoot through her body. It wasn't much longer before the three of them all came together.

CHAPTER 12

Marcus sat behind the wheel of another stolen car with Pony riding shotgun. Big Zo and another fellow junkie called Smokey took up the rear. The car was completely silent, each man consumed with his own thoughts. Getting high was the common theme, and just how to do it was what each man was pondering separately. Every once in a while, one of them would share his harebrained plan to get some money.

"Fuck it! I say we just run up in Walmart and run out with flat-screens," Smokey announced desperately.

"That's the dumbest shit I heard all day," Marcus spat, even though it had crossed his mind as well.

"We can hit ShopBrite. Red'll pay for meat," Big Zo pleaded eagerly.

"That's some ol' crackhead shit," Marcus said, his voice dripping with disgust.

"We crackheads!" Smokey said seriously.

"I ain't no crackhead," Pony shot angrily as the realization that he was indeed a junkie finally sank in. It wasn't supposed to be like that. He smoked a primo here and there with his best friend, and now he sat with that same friend scheming about what to steal. Pony looked over at Marcus in utter disgust. He instantly transferred all the blame to him. *Fuckin' wit' dis nigga*, he thought inwardly.

"What?" Marcus demanded, catching Pony's glare. "You got a better idea?"

"Naw, nigga, and I ain't robbing nobody," Pony shot back, rejecting the only idea Marcus suggested.

"Y'all fuck niggas is scared," Marcus fumed.

The men were all highly offended by the slanderous remark, but none felt like having Marcus point his gun at them, so they let it pass.

"Fuck it. We gonna hit the Walmart," Marcus commanded. "Big Zo, you make a commotion while Smokey hit up the DVDs. That should get us started."

No one made mention of the fact that Marcus had shot down this same plan minutes before. They knew the proceeds from the petty theft wouldn't quench the thirst of four heavy smokers, but desperation was sitting in.

* * *

Alonzo was recognized immediately upon entering the store. The manager instructed security to follow him while he called the police. They had enough surveillance footage of Big Zo ripping them off to put him away for a minute.

Smokey, with his classic junkie swagger and attire, was watched as well. Security cameras rolled as he loaded his clothes with loot. His description was passed along to the police officers who were en route to the location of the crime.

"Uh oh," Pony said as a cruiser pulled to an abrupt stop at the store entrance. "Let's push!" he said, nearly panicked.

"Be easy, nigga. It may not even be 'bout them," Marcus said, disgusted with the display of cowardice.

The words were barely out of his mouth when Smokey and Zo came bolting out of the store in a full run. Smokey was throwing the DVDs from his clothes at the pursuing guards. He was so focused on the guards behind him that he slammed head-on into the police officer responding to the call. The force of the impact sent them both sprawling on the ground, knocking the officer's weapon from his hand.

The officer scrambled for his gun, but Big Zo scooped it up before he could reach it. A second officer pulled to a stop just as Zo came up with the gun. For reasons no one will ever know, Zo pointed the weapon at its former owner and pulled the trigger. The heavy forty-caliber slug knocked the officer's hat off when it came out the back of his head. Alonzo then turned toward the second officer, closed his eyes, and began firing wildly.

When the shooting stopped, both Zo and Smokey, along with the cop, lay dead. The stray bullets that missed their mark killed a soccer mom who was there buying cleats for her boys.

"Go! Let's go!!" Pony shrieked, sounding more like an eight-year-old girl than a man.

This time, he got no argument from Marcus. "Man, did you see that shit!?" Marcus exclaimed excitedly. "Them niggas is dead."

"That's fucked up," Pony said, genuinely saddened by the loss of life.

"For real tho'," Marcus agreed, pissed because he wanted to kill something. "Man, how we s'pose to get high now?" Marcus said, getting back to more pressing matters. "Oh, I know!" he said, making a quick turn onto I-20. He was headed to P.I.G.'s with a plan to get credit. Everyone knew P.I.G. was addicted to drama, and having the inside scoop on what was sure to be make national news would be enough to gain entry. At the very least, Marcus was sure they'd be able to smoke as they recounted the night's events. *Hell, with a little acting, it might even warrant a little credit.* Truth be told, Marcus was thirsty enough to sweep up if he had to.

* * *

When P.I.G. took the call, his first instinct was to turn Marcus away, but since he'd just hung up from Tiffany, he changed his mind. Being the drama king he was, he decided to stage a little production of his own. "Hcy, fellas," P.I.G. said so genially that everyone looked up curiously.

"Oh, man! Did you hear?" Marcus began animatedly.

"Zo dem dead!" Pony jumped in, as rehearsed.

"Yeah, and dey kilt a po-lice. We had to shoot our way out of there," Marcus said.

"Wit' like ten cops," Pony embellished.

"Ten, huh? Sho nuff?" P.I.G. asked dubiously.

"They dead, man. They dead," Marcus said sadly, plopping down next to Mojo, who just happened to be loading his shooter.

Pony thought the display of remorse was a good look and adopted it as he laid out the fictionalized version of what went down.

"Damn. Sorry to hear that, fellas," P.I.G. said plainly.

"Worst part is dem niggas had the money we was gon' spend with you," Marcus said, setting the stage.

"Yeah. We had like ten stacks," Pony said, grossly overdoing it.

Marcus cringed at the obvious lie, but since it was in the air, he ran with it. "Yeah, so look...we gon' need you to hook us up with something on the face. Ima get it to you tomorrow," he asked confidently.

"Damn, man. I feel ya pain, but you know I don't do no credit," P.I.G. said as the opportunity to set his own plan in motion unfolded. Tiffany and Wanda would be arriving soon, so he had to move fast. "Tell you what I can do..." P.I.G. said, pausing for effect. "Y'all put on a little show, and I'll break ya off once you're done."

Marcus looked over at Stephanie, known to give the best head in three states, and agreed eagerly. He couldn't believe his good fortune: head and some gettin' high! "That's what's up!" he exclaimed, jumping to his feet. He was tugging at his zipper as he headed over to where Stephanie was sitting.

Stephanie, who would suck a dead man's dick for a hit, sat up in anticipation.

"Uh, that's not quite what I had in mind," P.I.G. spoke up. "I want you to suck his dick," he said, motioning toward Pony.

Marcus looked at Pony, then down to his crotch as if he was actually considering it.

"I ain't with no gay shit!" Pony spoke up angrily.

P.I.G. was pressed for time, knowing Tiffany would be there momentarily, so he enacted Plan B. "Gina!" he yelled loud enough to be heard in the rear.

A few seconds later, the handicapped girl appeared in one of the skimpy outfits P.I.G. kept her in to showcase her well-developed body.

"Go on and knock her off," P.I.G. demanded to Marcus, who wasted no time complying.

Pony felt sick to his stomach as he watch his friend slam

himself into the expressionless girl.

Marcus was so enthralled in the act that he didn't hear the knock on the door or Earl opening it.

"Hey, Tiff." P.I.G. chuckled. "There go Marcus."

It took Marcus a few more strokes for his mind to process what he'd just heard. He turned just in time to see Tiffany's back as she ran from the house.

"You a real piece of shit, P.I.G. You knew we was coming," Wanda spat at the obvious setup.

Meanwhile, Marcus went right back to humping the girl as if nothing had happened.

P.I.G. was immensely pleased with himself. *No way she'll go back with him now*, he thought to himself.

* * *

Back at the filthy hotel, Marcus and Pony frowned at the eight ball on the table.

"I should smoke this by myself since I did all the work." Marcus laughed, only half-joking.

"Man, something gotta give. We can't keep going out like dis." Pony sighed. The events of the night weighed heavily on his mind. People died. A child got molested. His best friend was ready to blow him. And for what? The eight ball on the table.

"All we need is one good lick, and we good," Marcus coaxed, sliding a chunk of the drug to Pony as an incentive.

"We could get a pack and do our thang, huh?" Pony asked as he loaded his shooter.

"Shit, nigga. We could get money, hoes, everything," Marcus said enthusiastically. Marcus wasn't sure if he heard his friend's reply properly and asked him to repeat himself.

"I said I'm down!" Pony repeated emphatically.

* * *

Marcus pulled the car in front of their intended victim's house and cut the engine. "You ready?" he asked.

Pony nodded his head in agreement.

"Nigga, I said, is you ready?" Marcus repeated, seeking a verbal commitment.

Instead, Pony pulled his ski mask down and got out of the car.

Marcus got out and followed him up the walk.

Red wasn't expecting anyone but rushed to the door nonetheless. Ever the businessman, he loathed the chance to miss a deal. He'd grown so comfortable with his personal rep and that of his sons that he thought no one would try him. It was that hubris that made him pull his door open without bothering to check and see who it was. Red realized his error immediately as the two masked men pushed their way inside, guns drawn. "You boys sure you want to do this? You do know who I am, right?" he asked warily.

"Shut up ol' man!" Marcus said forcefully as he shoved the man backwards.

"Yeah. You know what this is," Pony said, his voice strained with fear.

Red let out a heavy sigh as he reached into his pocket. "Here ya go," he said, producing a huge wad of cash that satisfied Pony instantly.

"I got it. Let's go!" Pony shouted excitedly after snatching the cash.

"Fuck dat. I want it all. Where da rest at, ol' man?" Marcus growled menacingly.

"Man…I know you!" Red announced, his face contorted by the recognition.

"You don't know me, nigga," Marcus stammered, attempting to drop his voice a few octaves.

"Come on, Marcus. We got the money," Pony said, nearly panicked.

"Marcus?" Red chuckled. "Boy, I thought that was you."

Marcus pulled the now-useless ski mask up and raised his gun. "Gimme da rest of dat dough," he demanded.

"What the hell you doing?" Pony asked desperately.

"Don't matter now. We might as well go all da way," Marcus said, inching closer.

It was at that instant that Red understood that Marcus intended to kill him. Being the A-Town vet that he was, Red sprang into action. He knew Pony was the weak link, so he went for his gun. Pony screamed as he and the older man wrestled for the weapon. Red was bigger and stronger than Pony and almost had him subdued until Marcus intervened. He calmly walked up to Red and literally blew his brains out the side of his head.

Pony screamed even louder as blood, bone, and brain matter splashed on his face and shirt. He felt his knees buckle and struggled to stay conscious.

"Come on! Let's find dis money!" Marcus demanded.

Pony followed Marcus into the master bedroom and began to search. Marcus dove into the large chest of drawers, while Pony hit the nightstand. They were tossing out the contents of the drawers, ransacking the room. It only took a couple of minutes before they hit pay dirt.

"Come on! I got it!" Marcus yelled, holding up another large wad of cash.

Pony abandoned his search inches short of where Red

had over $100,000 tucked away. The $10,000 Marcus found plus the $3,500 from Red's pocket was more than the junkies expected to find in the first place.

In a flash, they fled the house and pulled away from the murder scene.

Pony vacillated between rage and remorse, crying and cursing as they sped away.

Marcus, on the other hand, was eerily calm. The demons in his head were satisfied. They had been urging him to kill for months, and now he had. "You acting like a real bitch right now," Marcus said calmly. "Nigga, we 'bout to come up."

* * *

P.I.G. gave them the choice of buying a half a key of whipped cocaine for seven, or the same amount of the glass for eleven. They chose the latter. Most young cats would have gotten the whip even though the smokers didn't really like it. Being junkies themselves, they opted for the better product.

"Good choice," Earl said, congratulating their business decision. "Y'all 'bout to get rich with this," Earl said, completing the transaction. He knew that once the high-quality coke hit the streets, they would bubble quickly. He also knew they would fuck up just as quickly.

"Wonder who they robbed," P.I.G. said once they left.

"I'm sure we'll find out soon enough. They better never try us though," Earl replied.

"They know not to try me!" P.I.G. said smugly, confident in the fact that Earl would protect him, just like he always had.

CHAPTER 13

B oth women were in their respective rooms, preparing to go to work at the club. For Tiffany, that entailed selecting an outfit suitable for her first night in a strip club. Several outfits later, she settled on a pair of tight-fitting jeans and a matching shirt. After much debate, a pair of two-inch heels were given the honor of completing the ensemble. "You go, girl," Tiffany told the reflection in the full-length mirror. She took a hearty pull from her cocaine-laced blunt as she studied her figure. She did a little dance as she thought about how Wanda kept urging her to strip. "Uh-uh." She giggled shyly at the thought.

Wanda was preparing for the night as well. After a shower and a douche, she applied a high-priced fruity concoction from Victoria's Secret. She inhaled deeply, savoring the mango-peach aroma. Now that Tiffany would be bringing in some extra money, she planned to get strawberry-watermelon next.

She intended to squeeze the young girl for everything she could. Once she got her to dance, she would be open for anything. Then she and Mike could seduce her, easing the way for her to turn a few tricks. "Just a matter of time," Wanda told her reflection. "Just a matter of time."

She took a break from applying her make-up to load her straight shooter. The blunts just weren't doing it for her anymore. Wanda knew she had to be discreet about it because Mike would lose his mind if he found out she was on the pipe. He hated her smoking primos, even though he was the one who introduced her to cocaine and still snorted himself. He had lost too many girls to the pipe as it was. "What he don't know won't hurt him." Wanda shrugged before lighting her pipe. Her eyes grew large in the mirror as she twisted and turned the pipe under the flame. She held the smoke as long as she could before exhaling a putrid plume, then continued embellishing her pretty face.

* * *

Wanda suggested they take separate cars since she intended to spend the night at Mike's condo once the club closed for the night. Tiffany followed closely, consumed in her thoughts all the way up Moreland Avenue.

Club Chocolate was a small, nondescript, freestanding building across from a twenty-four-hour grocery store. Tiffany realized she must have driven by it a million times and not even noticed. At night, though, it stood out like a garish sore thumb, illuminated by a ton of tawdry neon lights.

It was far too early for the ballers who frequented the establishment to be out, so the parking lot was near deserted. Soon, though, the parking lot would hold millions of dollars' worth of exotic vehicles. A small section of the lot next to a side entrance was reserved for dancers. It was well lit and monitored by security cameras.

Wanda scoped Mike's new Porsche truck in front of the building. After parking, she and Tiffany walked around to meet him. As they approached, Mike was engaged in an animated conversation with the club bouncers. Tiffany blushed inwardly upon seeing Mike, remembering how she used his voice, his growls, to help her reach an orgasm the night before.

"Hey! There go my girls," Mike announced cheerfully when they came into view. He lifted Wanda up and planted a kiss on her lips.

"Mmm. Hey, yourself," Wanda purred, giddy from the affection.

"Hey, Mike," Tiffany gushed girlishly.

Mike had a sisterly hug for her as well once he sat Wanda down. He put one girl under each arm and led them inside. Tiffany, who was becoming intoxicated by the smell of his cologne and feel of his touch, melted into him.

The first thing that struck Tiffany as she toured the establishment was the smell. Over the cigarette and weed smoke, through the battle of warring perfumes and clashing colognes, and even the chicken being fried in the club kitchen could not compete. The place smelled just like pussy—not stank funky pussy, just a faint whiff of vagina. *No wonder*, Tiffany told herself as her eyes adjusted to the light. The place was full of women in various states of undress, all glistening with baby oil. Her self-esteem plummeted as she saw beauty after beauty. Just an hour before, she was admiring herself in her mirror, but now she wanted to run and hide.

Tiffany was lost in her thoughts as she entered this fascinating new world. She missed most of the narrative Mike gave, and before she knew it, she was back at the front door. Mike was still talking, but she had no idea what he was saying. "Excuse me?" Tiffany said, stopping him mid sentence.

Wanda sucked her teeth sarcastically, but Mike was more sympathetic. He recognized the deer-in-the-headlights stare in Tiffany's eyes, and he knew she was out of her element. "I said, this is where you'll be working," he repeated, pointing to the small booth where she would check ID and collect admission fees. "And sometimes my servers don't show up, so you'll have to help out there as well," Mike added.

Before leaving her at her post, he introduced her to Big D, the club's first line of defense. He protected against all adversaries, especially the dreaded broke niggers. They were the riffraff who sat in their cars getting as high as drunk as they could so they wouldn't have to pay for drinks in the club. It wasn't unheard of to catch one or more masturbating under the table. Big D would make sure to break an arm if he caught them.

"A'ight, lil mama. See ya later," Mike said with a wink before leading Wanda back into the bowels of the establishment.

Not long after Tiffany got settled in the booth, the customers came in droves. She saw plenty of familiar faces from school, work, and even church. For some reason, anyone who even remotely knew her asked what she was doing there. Wearied by the question, she began getting snippy as her patience wore thin. "What am *I* doing here?" she repeated curtly. "What are *you* doing here, Deacon Jones?"

The junior pastor from her church mumbled incoherently and slinked inside.

Big D looked at her with a raised eyebrow as if to say, *"What's up?"*

She caught herself, smiled at him brightly to indicate that

she understood, and went back to being cordial. After all, she knew what was wrong. She needed a blast. It had been almost an hour since she'd smoked, and that monkey on her back was growing restless. As it began to fidget, so did she. "Um, Big D, I left my inhaler in my car. Can you hold me down for a sec?" she asked sweetly.

Big D fell for the helpless routine and quickly agreed. "I got you," he said, assuming her duties.

Tiffany fought the urge to run to her car, where half a blunt waited in the ashtray. Walking as briskly as she was, she caught Mike's attention on the security monitor on his desk. She wasted no time once she entered her car. In a flash, she was taking furious drags on the cigar, holding the smoke for as long as she could. The monkey settled back down, and Tiffany outed the blunt again, making sure to save some for later.

Mike shook his head as he watched the whole episode on the monitor. He almost had second thoughts about turning her out until then. If she was smoking, selling some pussy was inevitable. *May as well get that money instead of someone else*, he reasoned.

He and Wanda had turned out hundreds of young women and girls. They had a stable of them working in clubs, private parties, escort services, and lately, even porno movies. The formula was simple: Wanda would get them using and then hand them over to Mike. Mike would put the dick on them and tell them he loved them. They would love him back and do whatever he asked of them to prove it.

Once the club was filled to capacity, Tiffany was asked to help serve drinks.

Ursula, the lone waitress for the night, showed her what to do. "Ima take the orders, and you just gotta brang dem they drinks," Ursula said in her heavy Southern drawl.

"Okay," Tiffany replied, staring wide-eyed in apprehension, nervous about actually going into the trenches.

"Ain't nothin' to it," Ursula said reassuringly, seeing the fear. "And we gon' split the tips."

It went smoothly, and Tiffany began to enjoy the attention she received. All the customers flirted with her, even while in the midst of a rump-shaking table dance. "Here you go," Tiffany said, handing over a tip for her and Ursula to split.

"A hunned dollars!?" Ursula exclaimed. "Dem cheap bastards neva gimme shit!"

"Guess cuz I'm new," Tiffany said naively.

Ursula shot her a cold glance until she realized she was serious. *Poor thing*, she reflected to herself, knowing Tiffany was too green to life to know that the only reason a man does anything for a woman is because he wants to fuck her—that "Good morning" and "How are you?" all translates to "Can I have some pussy?" Ursula shook her head knowing what was in store for her.

It was only a few years earlier that she was caught in Mike and Wanda's clutches herself. She'd met Wanda one day after moving to Atlanta from her family's southern Georgia farm. A week later, she had coke in her nose and a stranger's dick in her mouth. It took a year to shake off the yoke of drugs and get into school like she'd come for in the first place. Now, she only served drinks to make a living until she graduated.

She felt like telling Tiffany to run for her life, but she opted to mind her business. *She gonna have to learn the hard way... just like I did.*

CHAPTER 14

Marcus and Pony set up shop, armed with half a kilo of the best crack in town, bar none. While Pony weighed, cut, and bagged up the work, Marcus smoked it.

Pony wisely decided to sell it all in ten- and twenty-dollar increments to maximize profits. That entailed hella traffic and hella risk. Depending on how generous he felt, he could cut between $2,000 and $2,500 an ounce. He had eighteen ounces, which came to at least $36,000. *If dis nigga don't smoke it all first,* Pony thought as Marcus smoked rock after rock without a care in the world. *Nigga was ready to suck a dick.* Pony frowned at the memory. *You a junkie too, an inner voice whispered. You gon' be just like him if you don't stop.* It was at that exact moment that Pony decided to drop both bad habits real soon. Both Marcus and the dope had to go. "Here. Take these and give them out," Pony told Marcus, handing him the one-hit testers he'd bagged.

"*Give?*" Marcus asked, confused. "You mean for free?

"Yeah, give. Once the word get out that we got that glass, we straight," Pony said, giving him a brief lesson in marketing.

"That's what's up," Marcus agreed and set out on his task. He went room to room, smoking the testers with the other junkies.

The junkies were so used to the bullshit whipped cocaine that the renegades sold that they flipped once they got a hit of the butter. In fact, it set off a chain reaction that reverberated throughout the entire city. Those with cash came to cop, while those without cash went to get it. Shit got stolen, people got robbed, and dicks got sucked. The first customers came in a trickle, but that grew into an all-out flood. If there was a junkie dam somewhere, it had clearly broken.

Pony wisely rented two more rooms and switched at random, a plan devised to keep the jackers and police off balance.

A few customers complained about only being able to buy dimes or dubs, but Pony was in it to win it. As a concession, he let them get three for twenty-five or five for forty. Either way, he was winning. Before he knew it, the four ounces he'd bagged were gone. Pony initially thought he messed up somehow or Marcus cuffed some. Then he counted and re-counted the $7,500 stuffed in his pockets.

Marcus returned with a fine little smoker in tow. She was young and had to be a new convert since she still possessed all of her teeth, and she was thick where it counted. Marcus grabbed a handful of the dimes Pony was bagging and hand-ed a couple to the young girl. They both wasted no time in loading their pipes and lighting them. After a few hits a piece, they climbed on the bed and stripped naked. Marcus and the girl went at it as if they had the room to themselves, even as Pony served the customers that came and went.

Pony tried to ignore the copulating couple, but her moans were getting the better of him. "Say, what that hit like?" he finally asked.

"Come see for yaself," the young pro said. She changed positions so Marcus could hit her from the back while she accommodated Pony in her mouth. It only took the young pro a few minutes to get both men where they were trying to go.

* * *

By the next morning, the men had just over $13,000. It could have been more if not for Marcus's smoking and tricking. They still had eight more ounces stashed in the basement of Pony's grandmother's house. The plan was to flip that, then move up to a whole bird.

That was, of course, until Marcus saw all the money and had a change of plans. "Break me off," he demanded once the cash was counted.

"Be easy, shawty. We gon' flip it one more time before we pull anything out," Pony reasoned.

"Flip hell! Break me off!" Marcus insisted. "We got, what, thirteen stacks? That's at least four g's a piece," he said, flaunting his mathematical prowess. "I'm tryina ball, nigga!" He laughed.

Reluctantly, Pony forked over $6,200. He couldn't beat his old friend, but he did deduct a fee for what Marcus smoke, stole, and tricked with. In the end, he figured he was better off that Marcus wasn't interested in the goldmine they came across. He intended to flip his money to infinity. Niggers would die to get their hands on the quality of cocaine they had. He knew firsthand that at least one had died for them to get it.

A fool and his money, Pony mused inwardly as Marcus went store to store, trying his best to spend every dime. Pony realized he'd neglected himself in recent months and did a little shopping himself. He copped the newest Jordans, and Marcus bought three pair. Pony picked up a One Ummah jeans set, and Marcus got four. By the time they left the mall, Marcus had spent over $3,000 while Pony had only left a few hundred behind.

Pony did splurge a little, having his aunt rent a Cadillac truck for the weekend. He justified the expenditure by saying it was good for business, reasoning that if he had that much work, he needed to look the part. Truth be told, he wanted to floss a little bit too.

After a fresh cut and a hot shower, Pony felt like his old self and admired his new clothes.

Marcus still looked rough, despite the $1,000 outfit he wore. He stuffed $2,000 in his pockets to spend at the club, having every intention to make it rain!

Pony brought along $200 in cash and 100 one-hit testers. He was gonna make it rain, too, but in his direction.

* * *

Tiffany greeted the two men as if they were anybody off the street. "Welcome to Chocolate." She smiled genially at Pony, totally ignoring Marcus. A casual observer wouldn't have guessed that she ever knew Marcus, let alone that he'd been her first love.

"What the fuck you doing here?" Marcus demanded to know, ignoring the obvious.

Big D caught the outburst and took a step in their direction, until Tiffany waved him off. He did back off, but he continued to watch closely to see how she handled the situation.

"Tell your *little* friend that I work here," she said to Pony, still refusing to look at Marcus. Knowing how self-conscious Marcus was about his height, she went there again. "And tell your *little* friend the cover is twenty dollars per person," she said with a slight chuckle.

Pony tried his best not to laugh, but a small giggle escaped as he offered to pay.

"I got it!" Marcus shouted, pulling out his bankroll. "That ain't shit to a baller," he announced, tossing a C-note at Tiffany. "Keep da change, ho."

This time when Big D stepped forward to intervene, Tiffany was unable to wave him off. It was his job to prevent domestic squabbles like that one. Since so many dudes wanted to date strippers but couldn't handle it, he had his work cut out for him. The dudes would often post up at the bar mean mugging whoever "their girl" danced for. Whenever a situation got out of hand, they had to go, but there were two options—leave with or without getting their ass whipped first.

"It's cool, D. They alright," Tiffany said sternly, looking at Marcus for the first time.

"They better be," the bouncer growled. There was no mistaking the danger in his voice.

"Yeah, we cool," Pony said, dragging Marcus into the club before he could say anything else.

They found a couple of stools at the bar and mounted them.

Marcus made a big show of counting his money when he paid for the first round of drinks. "Say, shawty, let's get a table in the VIP," he announced loudly.

Pony glanced over at the VIP section and knew instantly that they were out of their league. The diamonds and platinum could be seen from across the room. "There go a table back there," Pony said, pointing toward the back. Marcus protested about wanting to be seen, but Pony knew better. The back of the club better suited his needs anyway.

Marcus gave Ursula a hard time when she delivered a bottle of champagne, but he tipped her well. She spread the word that there was a loudmouth showoff in the back, and the dancers made a beeline to break him. Marcus had three girls dancing for him at the same time, at twenty bucks a song each.

Pony made sure to slip each one a tester and his number. Once the girls realized what he'd handed them, they slipped off to sample it. The ones who didn't smoke kept them to trick with the girls who did smoke.

"Y'all got any more of dem thangs?" a dancer whispered in Pony's ear.

His first thought was to decline, as he intended to spread out the samples far and wide. That was until he looked up and got an eyeful of Jasmine.

Jasmine was a solid dime by anyone's standard. She was tall, red bone with rock-hard abs. Her breast stood out firmly, topped by pretty brown nipples.

Pony looked at her legs and wondered if she could dunk. When he saw her pretty lips twitching from the dope, he got hard instantly. "I'm getting low," he said, trying to keep his composure.

"Come on," Jasmine ordered, pulling him up by the hand. She led him upstairs to the private VIP rooms. "Gimme five minutes," she told a bouncer as she led Pony inside.

Once inside the room, Pony was inside her mouth before both cheeks touched the sofa he sat on. "This is the life!" Pony exclaimed, looking out the room window to the club below.

"Mmmhmm," Jasmine agreed at the same time fishing

the testers from his pockets as she blew him.

His enjoyment was threatened as he watched disaster unfold before his eyes. From his elevated vantage point, he saw Marcus stalking Tiffany with his eyes. She was delivering a tray of drinks to a table near his. He said something, she replied, and he jumped up, dumping the dancer off his lap. The girl screamed as she plummeted to the floor, alerting security of a problem. Then Marcus grabbed Tiffany by the arm and began yelling at her.

"Get the fu—" was all she got out before Marcus literally slapped the taste out of her mouth.

"This silly nigga," Pony fumed, watching the drama.

"What's wrong?" Jasmine paused to ask.

"Nothing," he replied, guiding her head back down.

Big D had been keeping an eye on Marcus and was the first to respond. When Marcus reared back to slap her again, his hand was caught by Big D's massive paw. He was joined by two other bouncers who dragged Marcus, kicking and screaming, to the rear exit. Mike had seen the incident from his office and went to investigate as well. Once outside, the bouncers literally tried to stomp a mud hole in his ass.

"A little to the left," Mike said, supervising the beat-down. "A'ight, that's enough," he commanded after Marcus was beaten thoroughly.

"Ima kill you," Marcus slurred, spitting saliva and blood on Mike's linen pants.

"Me?" Mike asked in disbelief after having just saved him from further abuse.

"Yeah, you," Marcus repeated, trying to rise to his feet.

"Well, take that with you," Mike said before kicking him in the mouth. The blow knocked out five of his front teeth. "Put this trash where it belongs," Mike said as he turned to leave.

The bouncers dragged Marcus to the large dumpster and tossed him.

Pony had finished off in Jasmine's mouth about the same time Marcus hit the bottom of the dumpster. He gave her a few more testers and told her to come by the hotel after her shift was over. He ran into Tiffany, who was still visibly shaken from being slapped. "You a'ight?" he asked sincerely.

"I'm cool. You need to be worried about your boy," she replied, feeling the welts that the slap caused.

"They ain't kill 'im, did they?" he asked casually, secretly hoping they did.

"Naw, but they shoulda," Tiffany spat.

"A'ight, shawty, I'll holla," Pony said, turning to leave.

"Say, I heard y'all got that fire," Tiffany said contritely. "You forgot about ya girl."

"My bad," Pony said apologetically, reaching into his pocket. He handed the rest of the testers to her with a wink. "Fuck wit' me," he said over his shoulder, going to retrieve his buddy. Pony almost passed by the dumpster until he saw Marcus peek out. "Hell, naw!" He chuckled, unable to contain it. He roared with laughter until they got back into the truck and he saw how badly Marcus was beaten. "Damn, cuz. You a'ight?" he asked sincerely.

"Ima kill dat nigga," Marcus vowed through his ravaged mouth. "I need a blast," he announced urgently.

"A blast!?" Pony inquired incredibly. "Shit, nigga, you need a doctor!"

Over Marcus's vehement objections, Pony steered the Escalade to Grady Memorial. On a typical Friday night, Grady would treat twenty or more gunshot victims, so a standard run-of-the-mill ass-whipping was a low priority.

However, once they got a look at the bruises and contusions Marcus sported, he was rushed into triage.

Marcus's mother, along with his sister and her kids, arrived twenty minutes after Pony called. They all waited in silence in the solemn hospital waiting room.

It was an hour before a doctor came out looking for family members. His grim demeanor unnerved the population of the waiting room full of praying friends and families. "Well…" the doctor sighed wearily from all the violence he'd witnessed that very same night. The corn-fed young Midwestern doctor could not believe how violent people could be. "He's got some head trauma, lost quite a few teeth, a good amount of blood, and several broken bones, but he'll live," he explained. The doctor went on to explain that Marcus would have to stay for observation to ensure no blood clots developed.

While Marcus's mother was worried, Pony was delighted to be free of the burden he was becoming, happy to have enough time to finish the package they had and a re-up. Without his partner smoking up half the work, he could maximize his profits. He resolved crack was to be sold, not smoked. He would pay Marcus his share of what was left and then go solo.

CHAPTER 15

"Fuck!" P.I.G. roared as the bad news was repeated on all local channels. A Mexican cartel operating in the city had been busted. Confiscated were hundreds of kilos of cocaine and millions in cash. They weren't just any Mexicans. These were his connect. The bust stemmed from the seizure of fifty keys the week before. Together, it meant one thing: drought!

Under normal circumstances, P.I.G. loved a good drought. As long as he was in pocket, he would make a killing. The problem was, he wasn't. The last of his traphouses just sold out, and he was catching hell trying to get back on. P.I.G. hated turning away money, but that was what he was forced to do, and he was in a foul mood as a result. The few junkies scattered around the room were feeling it as well.

He picked up the phone to call Blast again, but he changed his mind. He'd been calling her every five minutes since she left. She'd cursed him out thoroughly the last time, having grown impatient with his impatience.

Blast and Earl were out desperately trying to run down some dope. With her two-ounce-a-day habit, she was in no mood to be harassed.

P.I.G. had given her $30,000 to check some other dealers in town. Normally, putting that much cash in the hands of two smokers was begging to be ripped off, but he wasn't concerned in the least.

What almost no one knew was that shortly after rescuing young Blast from the clutches of her ruthless pimp, P.I.G. married her. They had to hire a junkie to pose as her mother since Blast was only fifteen at the time. She was the only woman P.I.G. ever had actual intercourse with. Blast even got pregnant once, but her polluted womb was no place to form life. They didn't have sex anymore, but she would blow P.I.G. several times a day if needed. Blast knew her husband was a trick. He would trick off every gram of product in the house if not for her. She was, by far, P.I.G.'s biggest asset, the driving force behind his accession up the ranks of Atlanta's drug dealers. She was the brains, and Earl was the muscle.

Earl was a known shooter, and as such, he didn't have to bust his gun much anymore. When you're known for shooting niggers, you don't get tried often.

Because of Earl and Blast, P.I.G. had five traphouses throughout the city, all doing big numbers. The two million dollars in the bank was due to Blast's business acumen.

P.I.G. knocked over his drink as he scrambled to answer his vibrating cell phone. "Yeah!?" he barked into the phone without bothering to check the caller ID.

"It's me. We straight. Be there in a minute," Blast said quickly before hanging up.

A wave of relief and excitement swept through P.I.G., causing him to summon his sex slave. "Gina!" he roared, loud enough to be heard in the back of the house.

Gina ambled out and went straight for P.I.G.'s exposed

penis.

The junkies in the room knew he must have scored and perked up, some passing gas loudly from the anxiety.

A knock on the door didn't disturb P.I.G. from the pleasure Gina was providing. "Get that!" he ordered without looking up.

"It Wanda dem," the junkie closest to the door announced after looking out the peephole.

"Let her in," P.I.G. growled reluctantly. He knew she despised him, and the feeling was mutual. If not for the business relationship he shared with Mike, he wouldn't even sell her a crumb. He hated the constant insults and the haughty way she turned her nose up at him.

True to form, Wanda sucked her teeth as she and Tiffany walked in. "Girl, that nasty fat bastard at it again," she hissed over her shoulder to Tiffany. "Where Blast? Let me cop so I can get da fuck outta here," she demanded with as much venom as possible.

"She ain't back yet, so you can push," P.I.G. spat back, matching her tone.

"We'll come back den," she said, turning on her heels.

"A'ight, but, uh…might be done sold out before you do," P.I.G. said, stopping her in her tracks.

Wanda was well aware of the shortage of cocaine in the city. The thought of going another day without a blast shook her to her very core. "Well, we'll just wait, then, if you don't mind," she said contritely.

P.I.G. knew what the upper hand looked like, and he knew he had it. He decided to take full advantage of it and make Wanda as uncomfortable as humanly possible. "Mmmm," he moaned loudly, grabbing the back of Gina's bobbing head. When he had everyone's full attention, he pulled out of

Gina's mouth and ejaculated. "Anyone want some of this?" he said, spewing semen all over the girl.

Tiffany fought the urge to throw up at the spectacle.

Suddenly, the front door swung open, stopping time in its tracks. Blast and Earl stormed in and headed straight to the back without saying a word. Their very presence set off another round of flatulence from the sofa.

P.I.G. got up as quickly as his massive weight would allow and followed them to the back.

Gina simply stared off into space as the semen ran down her face.

"Well? Whatcha get?" P.I.G. demanded, looking back and forth from Blast to Earl.

"One brick," Earl said solemnly, as Blast removed a kilo from her purse.

"And it's some bullshit," she added painfully.

"Desean charged you thirty stacks for a brick?" P.I.G. asked in disbelief.

"He charging more than that," Earl spoke up. "He let you get it for the thirty, and it's mediocre at best."

"You need to get back wit' dem New York dudes," Blast ordered. She caught her tone and attempted to clean it up before P.I.G. cursed her out.

"I'm saying though, Daddy, they got that raw, and the price is right," she purred sweetly. "We'll have the city on lock!"

"Humph, we'll see," P.I.G. responded, glaring at her. "Earl, I want you to put the whip on the whole thang."

"The whole thing?" Earl repeated, unable to mask the hurt in his voice. He could easily whip one key into to, but it was some bullshit.

"Hell, yeah. The whole thing!" P.I.G. barked. "I paid thirty for this. I gotta get mines back."

As he spoke, Blast separated an ounce that she no doubt intended to cook properly for her personal use. P.I.G. saw her do it, but he said nothing.

P.I.G. smiled brightly at the name on his caller ID. "What up, young balla?" he said when he flipped the phone open.

"I need to bump into you," Pony said desperately. He had all but cut Marcus off and was blowing up quickly. Marcus was allowed to hang around out of sheer loyalty, but that, too, was wearing thin. Pony threw him a little work every day, fully expecting him to fuck it up, and Marcus never let him down in that respect.

"Shit tight right now, but I got a little something. Gimme a minute to cook up," P.I.G. said before flipping the phone closed again. "Take twelve ounces to each house," P.I.G. told Earl, who was preparing to sample the freshly cooked batch. "And set aside four for that young nigger."

Earl and Blast both loaded large chunks of the pasty white product onto their shooters.

P.I.G. looked back and forth anxiously as they took long drags on their pipes. "Well? How is it?" P.I.G. demanded, causing Earl to blow out his hit sooner than he intended to.

"It's straight," he replied through a plume of noxious gray smoke.

"It'll do," Blast cosigned, blowing out her hit as well.

"Well, beggars can't be choosers," P.I.G. said arrogantly. "Tell them Js all we got is point five fifties."

Blast silently multiplied the $100 a gram they were charging by the 2,000 grams they had and smiled.

"Hurry up and make them rounds. We going to New York when you get back," P.I.G. ordered.

P.I.G.'s house was in full swing by the time Pony arrived.

He silently prayed he wasn't too late. There was no coke in the city, and if he could get on, he could really get rich. He had customers waiting to spend good money with him.

Wanda and Tiffany were pulling out as Pony pulled in. Marcus attempted to suck his teeth when Pony honked and waved at the women, but he didn't have any. Pony had to stifle a laugh at the resulting sound. The men sprinted toward the house, both hoping for the best, albeit for different reasons. A junkie opened the door, and they rushed inside.

"Where P.I.G.?" Pony asked breathlessly.

"In the back. Go on. He waiting on you," Blast replied.

Both men took off toward the rear until Blast stopped them.

"Just you," she said to Pony before lighting her pipe again.

Marcus made that strange sound again with his mouth and then plopped down on a sofa. He wistfully watched as everyone around him smoked. He was dying for a blast, but nobody shares in a drought.

"Come on!" P.I.G. shouted in response to the knock on his door.

"What it do?" Pony asked, looking around as he entered P.I.G.'s inner lair. "Damn!" he exclaimed at the sheer elegance of the room. It was unexpectedly extravagant. His Jordans sank up to the ankle in the plush white carpet.

Gina was laid out on the huge custom bed, wearing a sexy nightie, looking like a Special Olympics version of Lil Kim.

The room contained all the latest audio-visual equipment all run by a huge remote control unit.

"I need a whole one," Pony said, looking up at his reflection in the mirrored ceiling, pulling out cash from the pockets of his designer jeans.

P.I.G. took note of the expensive clothes Pony wore and

nodded in approval. He had to admire the hustle the young man had. He'd quit smoking and totally transformed himself. The dingy clothes he wore were replaced by Polo and Gucci. The stolen hoopties they pushed were swapped for a new Tahoe sitting royally on twenty-eight-inch rims. "You know shit tight right now," P.I.G. replied. "Best I can do is a couple of zones for a stack a piece, and it's that whip," he added, almost apologetically.

"Damn, P.I.G.! A stack? For whip?" Pony whined.

"Who else got dope besides me and now you?" P.I.G. asked.

"Ain't nobody got nothing," Pony admitted.

"That's right. Nobody got nothing," P.I.G. repeated. "So you charge a dollar a gram? Niggers got no chance, either pay it or stay sober, and you know they ain't tryina stay sober."

Pony quickly figured out he could at least triple his money. P.I.G. sold him four and a half ounces for $4,000, giving him a slight discount, and Pony thanked him profusely before turning to leave.

"Oh, and one more thing…" P.I.G. said, stopping Pony as he hit the door. "If you really wanna get rich, you gonna hafta lose that deadweight."

CHAPTER 16

T iffany felt like crying as she looked at the small amount of coke her money got her. She spent her last $100 and had only a gram to show for it. Being relatively new to the dope game, she didn't understand the mechanics of a drought. Had she not been there, she would have sworn Wanda had cheated her. She was used to getting an eight ball for sixty and spoiled the extra gram or two P.I.G. would throw her. Tiffany felt a swell of anger as she watched Wanda cut large chunks from the package she had, knowing her money paid for it.

Wanda had been literally milking her dry since she came to stay with her. Every day, she had her hand out for something—$50 for the light bill, $80 for the gas, $100 for this, and $200 for that. When Wanda found out that Mike would toss her a few extra bucks here and there, she went after that as well. The attention Mike showed Tiffany was making her jealous.

The plan, tried and true, was to leave the girls broke, forcing them to strip and trick. Wanda's blood began to boil as a drug-induced paranoia suggested that Tiffany must be trying to take her man. In an instant, she began to hate her young protégé, but she was far too shrewd to show it. "Phase Two," Wanda said to herself as she pulled out her straight shooter in front of Tiffany for the first time. It was time for Miss Goody Two Shoes to earn her stripes. She felt the young girl's eyes glued to her as she loaded a large piece of crack onto the pipe. Wanda twisted and turned the shooter dramatically as the flame danced on its tip, filling the quiet room with a loud sizzle.

Tiffany watched in awe as a steady stream of smoke rushed from the tip into Wanda's mouth.

"Humph!" Wanda said desperately, causing a sense of urgency as she handed Tiffany the pipe.

Not knowing what else to do, Tiffany took it and inhaled. The effect was immediate, intense, and irreversible. As any junkie would tell you, there is nothing—nothing!—like that first hit. The rest of Tiffany's crack career would be spent trying to duplicate that first hit, that first high.

The two women smoked in silence until time drew near to go to the club.

"Guess we best get ready to go." Tiffany sighed, looking at her watch. In her heart, she felt like just smoking the night away.

"So what's up? You ready to hit that pole?" Wanda asked for the hundredth time. Every night over the past couple of weeks, Wanda had propositioned Tiffany to take the stage, and every night, the answer was the same…until now.

Tiffany was almost as surprised by her answer as Wanda was.

"Excuse me!?" Wanda exclaimed, incredulous.

"I said, yeah, I'm ready," Tiffany replied curtly as she headed for her room.

A lifetime of lessons ran through Tiffany's mind as she showered. "Sit properly," "Act like a lady," "Respect yourself," reverberated in her head as she prepared to disregard everything she'd been taught. She fought the urge to masturbate as she showered. Tiffany reflected on her limited sexual experiences,, which until now consisted of the handful of times she and Marcus had done the deed, and of course her recent affair with her finger and showerhead. "I need some dick!" she announced, turning off the water.

As Tiffany dressed, she entertained herself by doing a few moves in front of the mirror. She had picked up quite a few moves by watching the girls in the club.

A knock on the door interrupted her routine, and Wanda peeked in. "You ready, lil mama?" she sang, handing her the loaded shooter. Wanda wanted to keep her primed up so she wouldn't have a change of heart.

"Hell, yeah! Let's ride!" Tiffany exclaimed, eagerly accepting the offering.

* * *

"You can ride with me since Mike got some business," Wanda announced.

Once in the car, Wanda handed Tiffany a small white pill. "Here, girl. This'll make you feel sexy," she said as Tiffany plucked it from her hand.

"What is it?" Tiffany asked after washing it down with her soda.

"X. Yo lil ass gon' be rolling good in a minute," Wanda chuckled. Wanda pulled over a few blocks before the club, and they shared a quick blast.

Mike was holding court out front as the women pulled up.

After parking, they went around to meet him. Wanda felt a swell of anger as Mike greeted Tiffany before greeting her.

"Lil Ms. Thang ready to hit the stage," Wanda announced dryly.

"So nuff!" Mike gushed enthusiastically. "Make sure y'all call me. I don't want to miss this."

Tiffany was a nervous wreck as she waited for her turn onstage. She downed shot after shot of Alizé, attempting to settle down. The X she had taken earlier was now shooting waves of electric sexual energy through her body with every heartbeat. Remembering the loaded straight shooter Wanda had left in the ashtray, Tiffany slipped out for a quick blast. The effects of all the drugs coursing through her system were almost overwhelming.

Just as she slinked back into the club, her name was announced as next up. After a quick once-over in the dressing room mirror, Tiffany floated to the stage. She was so high her feet barely touched the floor.

A stir of commotion rang around the club when the regulars realized that Tiffany, now known as "China Doll," was dancing. Over the months, she had turned all of them down for dances, drinks, and dates, so her being onstage was a big deal.

The DJ threw on the latest D-lite song, and Tiffany began moving to the beat.

Wanda squeezed her way to the front to watch and coach her protégé.

Mike, too, had come down from his office perch to watch from the side of the stage.

The DJ announced that $200 would get China Doll out of the sexy boy shorts she was wearing. No sooner than the words left his mouth, hundreds of dollars were stretched toward her.

Wanda motioned for Tiffany to go around and collected the outstretched bills. Naively, Tiffany took the first bills in her hand until Wanda caught her attention. She lifted her leg and snapped her garter belt, reminding Tiffany to let the patrons place their money there.

Tiffany danced over to a twenty-dollar bill and dipped low enough for its previous owner to put it in her garter. The man's hand rubbed against her crotch, causing her knees to buckle slightly as a wave of electric sexual energy pulsed through her body again.

It seemed that every customer managed to brush against her crotch as they filled her garter belt. By the time she removed the boy shorts, they were soaking wet.

A few hundred dollars more, and Tiffany was as naked as the day she was born. The excitement of the drugs, alcohol, and men touching her was too much for her. She was in a zone as she leaned against the pole, gyrating with the music and rubbing her rock-hard nipples.

Tiffany lost track of her surroundings as she got caught up in the sensation she was giving herself. She slid down the pole until she was squatted with her legs wide open. Oblivious to the crowd and needing to get off, she began to masturbate.

The club grew eerily quiet, as the DJ got so caught up in the show that he neglected to put another song on. The only sounds to be heard were Tiffany's whimpers as she neared an orgasm.

Tiffany couldn't contain herself any longer and let out a scream as the powerful climax wracked her body. Her legs came out from under her, leaving her spread eagle on the stage, exposing her dripping vagina.

The club was still, and not even the chirp of a cricket could be heard.

"Hell, yeah!" someone yelled, causing the club to erupt.

Tiffany was totally embarrassed as she came back to the reality of her surroundings. Through a rain of bills, she saw hundreds of smiling faces. Only one face wasn't smiling. In fact, its owner looked mortified. Tiffany squinted to bring the shocked face into focus. It was her turn to be shocked once she recognized Carlos. She sprang to her feet and bolted from the stage.

When she made it to the dressing room, Tiffany collapsed on a bench. She was just so embarrassed. She wished she could just disappear.

Just as she made up her mind to get dressed and go home, another dancer came in with a bucket of cash. "Gurrl… you…turned that shit out!" Diva exclaimed.

Tiffany was confused by the money but accepted it. "Um…thank you," she mumbled, looking at what had to be thousands of dollars, not to mention the garter she wore was also stuffed with cash.

Soon, the other dancers flowed in, all echoing Diva's sentiments.

"Girl, they still tripping out there!" one yelled.

"Ima do dat same shit," exclaimed another.

All the girls congratulated Tiffany except one. Wanda was absolutely fuming at the thought of being shown up. It was her man's club, and she was the star, the headliner. To make matters worse, she saw how Mike reacted to the performance.

"What the hell is going on back here?" Mike boomed as he made his way into the crowded dressing room. "This s'pose to be a strip club, and all the strippers in here! Y'all get y'all asses back on the floor," he commanded.

The room emptied before all the words exited his mouth.

The only people left were Tiffany, Wanda, and Mike.

"You! Come with me," Mike demanded, looking at Tiffany.

"You want me to come too?" Wanda pleaded.

"Nah. Go dance," Mike replied without even bothering to look in her direction.

Wanda shot Tiffany a dangerous glance as she rushed to catch up with Mike. She knew full well Mike intended to sex her after that nasty little show of hers. "I got you," Wanda spat at Tiffany's departing back. "Yeah, I got you."

* * *

"Close the door and lock it," Mike demanded as he entered his office with Tiffany in tow.

She did as ordered but stayed by the door, afraid she was in trouble. She'd heard Mike complain time after time about the vice squad spying on him. One girl had been arrested the week before for solicitation. Tiffany clutched at her robe just knowing she was about to be fired.

"Come around here," Mike ordered in a softer tone as he sat at his desk.

Tiffany, still fearful, didn't budge. When Mike began to unbutton his shirt, it became clear what he wanted. Tiffany decided in an instant that she was going to give it up to him.

When she came around the desk, Mike picked her up and placed her on the desk in front of him. He opened her robe and then laid her back and spread her legs. To Tiffany's surprise, Mike buried his bearded face in her crotch. By now, he knew enough of Tiffany's sexual and hygiene habits from Wanda and had no qualms about going down on her.

Tiffany, who had never experienced oral sex and considered it to be gross, came in seconds. When Mike's tongue slipped inside of her, she was shocked that it felt as large as Marcus's penis.

Mike kept licking her until another strong orgasm shook her small body. When she came, she emitted a spray of juices that splashed Mike's face. When he stood up, his beard was literally dripping.

Remembering how, at the dentist, looking at the needle was always worse than the actual shot, Tiffany told herself not to look as Mike removed his pants. She regretted not taking her own advice when she saw the huge penis in front of her. It looked to be the same size as his leg.

Mike lined himself up and pushed forcefully inside of her. Tiffany screamed as he filled her up, then again when she came for the third time. A few strokes later, Mike screamed as he let go inside of her. Through the pain, Tiffany was quite pleased with herself when the large man slumped on top of her, breathing heavily.

Wanda had heard enough from the door and removed her ear. Blinded by tears, she ran to her car without even bothering to change into her street clothes.

When Mike's breathing returned to normal, he ordered Tiffany to get dressed to leave. He called his assistant manager and told him he was leaving for the night.

Sam, the assistant, understood; he'd seen the show as well.

Tiffany would have to get the tour of Mike's swank Buckhead condo some other time. As soon as they entered, he practically dragged her to the rear. The plush furnishings and 1,000-gallon fish tank filled with colorful creatures were just a blur.

Mike's bedroom walls were painted black to match the carpet, curtains, and furniture. He turned on a black light that bathed the room in a gothic glow. "Go on. Knock that out,"

Mike said, handing her a black plate with neat white lines of powder cocaine.

Tiffany longed for a blast, but this would have to do.

He popped a pill and swallowed it with a large shot.

"What's that? X?" Tiffany inquired giddily between snorting lines.

"Uh-uh. Viagra," Mike replied with a wicked grin. He almost felt sorry for the young girl, knowing what was in store for her.

When Mike began to feel the effects of the Viagra and the liquor, he stripped Tiffany and then himself, and everything was underway.

* * *

The next morning, Tiffany's vagina was so battered and swollen she couldn't even put her panties back on.

Mike got a kick out of watching her limp around his apartment. "You a'ight? Sprain yo' ankle or something?" Mike giggled as they made their way to the elevator.

"Ha ha," Tiffany replied, poking out her lip.

"How much did you make last night?" Mike inquired, sounding businesslike.

"Um…almost $2,000," Tiffany answered, a little taken aback by the change in his demeanor.

"I know you was in a hurry last night, so make sure you bring your 10 percent when you come tonight. You'll do a lot better once we get you a few table dances," Mike rambled on with dollar signs in his eyes.

Tiffany chided herself internally for allowing herself to think last night meant something. "Yeah, I guess so," she said sadly.

Mike wasn't new to the game. He heard her tone and knew she needed to feel special right then. The young ones were like that. He'd been turning girls out on some level since third grade. "This is just the beginning for us," Mike said, pulling her close. "I have much bigger things in store for us." Mike planted a soft kiss on her forehead to punctuate the word "us." The girls liked that word; it made them feel included.

"Mmm. Bigger than this?" Tiffany asked, playfully grabbing his manhood.

"Don't start nothing you can't finish," Mike warned, reacting to her touch.

Tiffany felt a stab of pain in her crotch when Mike began to stiffen in her hand. She quickly pulled away, fearful of dealing with that monster again so soon.

Mike got a good laugh out of the horrified look on her face and teased her about it.

They were so caught up in their playful banter that they walked right past Marcus, who was slumped down in a stolen car. He'd followed them from the club the night before and spent the night smoking in the parking lot. Marcus smoked and plotted, plotted and smoked. He fully intended to make good on his promise. Tiffany had just been added to his list.

CHAPTER 17

"Why they won't just deliver it like they used to? Why you gotta go way up there?" Blast grumbled as she re-counted the money.

"They say they need to talk to me," P.I.G. said more confidently than he felt. He'd been wondering the same thing. P.I.G. knew his New York connection was salty when he abruptly changed suppliers. The Mexicans had the same grade of cocaine at a better price than the Dominicans he dealt with in New York. Once Atlanta was established as a major distribution city, New York felt the pinch.

"One fifty," Blast announced as she neatly stacked the cash inside a tote bag.

P.I.G. traded the raggedy sweatpants he generally wore around the house for a tailored suit. The Dominicans, although ruthless drug dealers, were very formal. Blast had selected a charcoal-gray suit and set it off with black gators and a matching belt. A gray brim covered the intricately designed braids Blast had just completed.

"Get Gina ready. I'm taking her along for the ride," P.I.G. demanded as he admired himself in the mirror.

"Don't bring her back!" Blast demanded in a tone she rarely used. She had begun to despise the young girl since her husband seemed to prefer Gina's mouth to hers.

P.I.G. heard the bitterness in her tone and knew Gina's time had come. "Maybe I can sell her," P.I.G. offered, hating to let her go. She was, after all, payment for a debt. He started to argue that point, but then he thought better of it.

Being as large as P.I.G. was, a plane was out of the question—not that he would have flown anyway because he was afraid of flying. Earl pulled his boss's custom SUV in front of the house and waited. Besides the custom paint and rims, the truck also boasted a state-of-the-art entertainment system including a thirty-two-inch plasma TV, satellite dish, and over twenty speakers. All of the middle and rear seats were removed and replaced by a large loveseat, custom-made to accommodate P.I.G.'s vast size.

P.I.G. checked the street carefully before making his way to his vehicle. He clutched the bag containing $150,000 closely to his side.

Gina, in one of her seductive outfits, ambled behind him, looking like Nicki Minaj.

Once everyone was settled inside, Earl and P.I.G. prepared themselves for the long ride. For Earl, that meant having his shooter and an ample supply of rocks close at hand.

Meanwhile, P.I.G. pulled out his penis and summoned Gina. He had to call her again to break the trance the outside world engulfed her in. As soon as she saw his exposed penis, she made her way to it, just as she was trained.

"Let me know if you want some of this," P.I.G. snorted, offering Gina to Earl for the hundredth time.

"Naw, I'm cool," Earl said, declining for the hundredth time as well.

"Don't let me find out you don't like women no mo'," P.I.G. said, roaring with laughter.

"I get a lot more than you think I do," Earl shot back with enough hostility to make P.I.G. leave him alone…for now.

* * *

Following the GPS navigation system, Earl pulled in front of the suppliers' building in just over thirteen hours. They could have made better time if not for P.I.G.'s addiction to Mickey D's. Every time he saw those golden arches, he demanded that Earl pull over.

"We're here, boss!" Earl repeated again, louder to wake the snoring, slobbering man.

Once P.I.G. was fully awake, they exited the vehicle, leaving Gina behind to chase the incoherent thoughts through her crippled mind.

A runner greeted P.I.G. and Earl warmly and escorted them into the building.

The Washington Heights section of Harlem was one of the most dangerous places on Earth, unless you were there to do business with the Dominicans; then it was one of the safest.

"Don Carlos, he is very happy to see you," the runner smiled as the elevator rose. Once they reached the third floor, the smile disappeared from the man's face, and his demeanor changed. "You stay with me," he ordered Earl, who looked at P.I.G. for approval.

P.I.G. gave a nod and then went inside.

"*Mi amigo!*" Don Carlos exclaimed, jumping to his feet. He rushed over and shook the large man's hand.

"Uh, what's up?" P.I.G. asked, a little confused. He fully expected to be scolded for jumping ship the way he did.

"Please sit," Don Carlos said, pointing to a circa-1970s sofa still wrapped in thick plastic.

A worker came out of a back bedroom and reached for P.I.G.'s bag of cash. P.I.G. was hesitant until Don Carlos gave a reassuring nod. The worker took the money to be counted as P.I.G. and Don Carlos made small talk.

"Very sorry to hear about your Mexican friends," Don Carlos said unsympathetically. In fact, it was he who fed them to the Feds. It was part of the dirty game they played. Don Carlos considered himself merciful for turning them in instead of murdering them as his partners suggested.

The men negotiated to have twenty kilos of cocaine shipped once a week, same as before, except for a $1,000-per-bird penalty. P.I.G.'s disloyalty was going to cost, and the next fee would be his life.

Once the transaction was complete, Earl was allowed to enter to carry the twenty-three pounds of coke to the truck.

Don Carlos and P.I.G. exchanged niceties that neither truly meant and then said their goodbyes.

"Say, you wanna buy a sex slave?" P.I.G. offered at the door.

"Excuse me?" Don Carlos asked in confusion.

"A sex slave. She do anything. She retarded. I got her in the truck right now," P.I.G. said proudly.

"I'll have to pass. I'm afraid my wife would not approve," Don Carlos replied apologetically.

* * *

Back in the truck, Earl lined up hits of crack on the dashboard for the trip. P.I.G. got another blow job and was asleep before they hit the George Washington Bridge.

Five hours later, Earl pulled into a Mickey D's in Washington DC, as instructed.

"Right there! Right there!" P.I.G. squealed as the iconic arches came into view.

"The usual, boss?" Earl inquired as he prepared to exit the truck.

"Yeah, and take Gina inside for a Happy Meal and leave her happy ass," P.I.G. replied.

"Leave her?" Earl repeated, not sure if he heard correctly. "In there?"

"Yeah, in there, nigga! What? You Captain Save-a-ho now?" P.I.G. barked. "You can stay with her if you want."

"Come on, Gina. Eat," Earl said solemnly. He hated having to do that to the girl. He tried to comfort himself by pretending someone would take her in, though the chances were that in that neighborhood, in that outfit, she would almost certainly be victimized further.

It was at that moment that Earl decided to kill P.I.G. He and Blast had talked about it several times over the last few months—every since he'd forced them to have sex with each other.

Once, on a slow night, he ordered Earl to fuck his wife in her ass.

"This coochie mine, but can have the ass," P.I.G. said with a sickening chuckle as he taped the episode. Whenever he felt like humiliating one or both of them, he'd play the tape for the junkies in the room.

What P.I.G. didn't count on was that Evil and Blast were catching feelings for each other. He was far too arrogant to believe that the help could take his wife. They both realized life could be for the better without P.I.G. in it.

"Your days are numbered," Earl swore as he led the

handicapped girl to be stranded. "Time's almost up!"

* * *

When they arrived back in Atlanta, P.I.G. was wide awake…and wide open.

"A'ight. Let's get this money," P.I.G. announced to Blast when they entered the house.

"Where's your retard?" Blast asked when she didn't see Gina.

"What's it to you?" P.I.G. snapped, still bitter about having to give her up. "You need to start cooking and stay out my business. I want y'all to whip a bird for each house, and stick with the fifties," P.I.G. ordered, fully intending to milk the drought for all it was worth. "Earl, run over and check the traps. Bring back the money so we can make another move.

Earl, who had just driven for over twenty-seven hours straight, followed orders without complaint.

* * *

Pony was enjoying the back of Diva's throat so much that he almost ignored his vibrating phone. "Oh shit!" he exclaimed, startling Diva off the wood. "Tell me something good, big homie," Pony said as he eased Diva's head back down.

"Eighteen for a whole one," P.I.G. said warmly, "and it's that glass."

"That glass? Eighteen?" Pony repeated, enthused. He made a nice lick off the couple ounces of whipped dope, but his customers were grumbling.

"Come on," P.I.G. said urgently.

Diva knew coke talk when she heard it and worked her

neck a little harder.

"I'm coming!" Pony yelled to both P.I.G. and Diva.

CHAPTER 18

Tiffany re-counted her stash and could not believe the tally. Even smoking a quarter of an ounce a day, she still managed to squirrel away $10,000. Her freak show propelled her to the top spot at the club. It was beyond belief that men paid so much for her to get herself off. She was now the headliner, the position once held by her housemate.

The spotlight wasn't the only thing Tiffany stole from Wanda. Mike now took her home three or four nights a week, while Wanda got none. Oddly enough, Wanda didn't trip. However, her behavior became more erratic by the day as her cocaine consumption grew to Blast-like proportions.

Tiffany had set a goal to move once she reached ten stacks. Now that she had achieved it, it was time to bounce.

Mike had been promising to let her move in with him, but Tiffany couldn't wait on him. After she put her money back in the shoebox that doubled as a safe, she set out to Mike's.

I wonder what this "big favor" is, Tiffany mused to herself, mocking Mike's voice. He had called and told her to drop everything and rush over, and that was exactly what she did, speeding to get there.

She was now head-over-heels in love with Mike, and she knew he felt the same. He just never said it, though he was always talking to her about "us" and "our future."

"Yeah, he love you, girl," she told her reflection in the elevator as it took her upwards. When she arrived at his floor, she glided down the hallway and rang the bell.

"Damn, you made it quick," Mike said in astonishment. He pulled the door open wide and ushered her inside.

"I told you I'm here for you whenever you need me," Tiffany told him, meaning every syllable. "So what's this big favor?" she asked as they sank onto the plush leather sofa.

For a response, Mike leaned back and pulled out his semi-erect penis.

"My, that IS a big favor!" Tiffany chuckled as she stood to undress.

"Uh huh," Mike said, pulling her back down. He gently caressed her neck, guiding her head down toward his growing erection.

"Nooo, babeeey. I told you I don't do that," Tiffany cooed. She had refused to go down on him, no matter how many times he made her cum with his tongue. The firm grip on her neck told her refusing wasn't an option anymore. "I don't even know how to do it," she said, kissing the throbbing head. Finding it nowhere near as repulsive as she thought it would be, she kissed it some more.

"Mmmm, baby. I love you so much," Mike said, causing her lips to spread. When they did, he pushed his way inside.

Tiffany had witnessed countless blow jobs at P.I.G.'s and the club, so she mimicked what she saw. She was soon working her head and hands like an old pro.

Mike slid a hand under her miniskirt and pushed a finger past her panties. They both moaned loudly as they pleased each other. A few minutes later, they came together. When Mike exploded in her mouth, he held her head in place, forcing her to take every drop. When he relaxed his grip, Tiffany took off for the bathroom like she had been shot out of a cannon.

Mike slumped back on the sofa as Tiffany spat, rinsed, gargled, brushed, rinsed, and spat some more. Five minutes later, she emerged, pouting with her arms folded across her chest.

"So that…was your big favor?" Tiffany asked with far more attitude than she felt.

"Actually, that is a part of it," Mike replied, pulling her down next to him. "I have a very important client on the way, and I need to impress him. This is the break we need," he said urgently.

"What do you need me to do?" Tiffany asked, eager to please.

"Exactly what you did just now," he responded. "Fuck him, suck him, whatever he wants."

The doorbell rang just as Tiffany opened her mouth to protest.

"Whatever he wants!" Mike said again before opening the door.

The visitor was a handsome light-skinned guy about Mike's size and age. The two men greeted each other warmly with the standard pound and man-hug.

"Tiffany, meet John. John, Tiffany," Mike said by way of introduction.

"Hey, John," Tiffany said shyly as John came over to shake her hand.

"Hey, yourself, cutie," John said eagerly as he took her small hand into his. "Damn, Mike. You said she was fine, but damn!" John exclaimed.

"Well, if you two will excuse me, I got a quick errand to run. Tiff, keep John comfortable till I get back," Mike said on his way out the door.

The door closed before Tiffany had a chance to say anything. Now she was all alone with a stranger. She hoped John didn't know what was expected of her. *Maybe I can just kick it with him, flirt a little till my man come home.*

Her hopes were soon dashed as John began to undress.

Not knowing what else to do, Tiffany undressed and let the stranger have his way with her. To cope with it mentally, Tiffany pretended to be someone else. She was freaking John every which way but loose. In the hour they were alone, she had done everything sexually that she'd done in her life. If pleasing him was pleasing Mike, then Mike should have been thoroughly pleased, because John was spent.

When Tiffany returned from rinsing her mouth out again, John was fully dressed. "Thanks, babe," John exclaimed, extending his hand. "That was great."

Tiffany thought it odd to shake hands after all they had done, but she didn't want to be rude. When she took his hand, it was full of cash. She looked at him in confusion but said nothing.

John thanked her again and then disappeared through the door.

Tiffany was still standing there holding the cash when Mike returned minutes later.

"How'd it go?" Mike asked enthusiastically.

"Okay, I guess," Tiffany replied, still confused as to what just happened. "He gave me money," she said, showing Mike the wad of bills.

"Great! Go buy yourself something nice," he replied. He watched with delight as Tiffany put the money in her purse, having officially turned her first trick. It would, however, be the last time she kept the money. "Okay. Well, I got some things to do, so I'll see you at the club later," Mike said dismissively.

Tiffany got the hint that it was time to go, so she did.

As soon as the door closed behind her, Mike whipped out his cell phone and dialed. "John pleased," Mike said with a chuckle as his friend Will answered.

"Ooh wee! Nigga, you got a goldmine. Shawty is all that," Will exclaimed.

"Oh, I know it! Got them old niggas lined up at $2,500 a pop," Mike gushed.

"Shit! I got off cheap for that $500 I gave her." Will laughed.

"Yeah, especially since it was my $500," Mike said, joining the laughter.

CHAPTER 19

Wanda knew her life was spiraling out of control but was powerless to stop it. She had no brakes, and rock bottom was rushing toward her at 100 miles an hour. The rage inside her boiled as she thought about her situation. The young girl she had taken in to help out had, in turn, helped herself to her job and her man. Lately, Mike had been acting as if he hardly knew her. She'd lost her headliner spot at the club and was reduced to just being one of the dancers. As the featured performer, Tiffany was pulling in thousands; Wanda, on the other hand, only brought home hundreds.

Tiffany was now paying all the bills because Wanda smoked away every penny she earned. She couldn't give a fuck about a light bill or the cable. To make matters worse, the little ingrate was even talking about moving out.

A plot took shape in Wanda's head as she drained the last bit of smoke from her pipe. Before even exhaling, she sprang into action. She began tossing pillows off the sofa and scattering items haphazardly around the room. Wanda unhooked the TV and DVD player and placed them by the door. She then tossed her own room and placed the valuables by the front door as well.

Having no idea when Tiffany might return, Wanda moved quickly in her room. She made a beeline to the closet and the brand-new Coogi tube dress Tiffany just got. "Gotcha!" Wanda said to the dress as she plucked it from the stuffed closet. Of course the dress was too small for her, but she still didn't want Tiffany to have it. Tiffany had made a big show of the dress when she brought it home, making sure to show Wanda the $1,500 price tag and let her know that Mike's money had paid for it.

Her anger grew as she came across item after item in the closet with tags still attached. She couldn't wear any of it, but Tiffany wasn't going to either if she had anything to say about it.

She couldn't help but admire Tiffany's taste in shoes as she dumped them from their boxes. Wanda had to do a double-take as thousands of dollars fell out of one of the boxes. The thought of how much dope she could buy caused Wanda to fart loudly. She was laughing and farting as she stuffed the money in Tiffany's new Prada purse.

She quickly loaded her car with the stolen loot and pulled off. If she'd taken a right instead of a left, she would have passed Tiffany heading home. Since left was P.I.G.'s direction, she missed her.

* * *

Tiffany always felt a little dirty after taking a client, so after the three men she'd serviced that day, she felt absolutely filthy. She had her heart set on a hot bath and a blast, and not necessarily in that order.

A sinking feeling came over her as she pulled into the

driveway and saw the front door ajar. "Oh, what now!?" she said aloud, wondering what kind of stunt Wanda had cooked up. Every day it was something. "Hello?" Tiffany called out cautiously as she pushed open the front door.

She was gripped instantly by panic when she saw the ransacked room. She ran on shaky legs to check her room and more specifically, her stash. Despite all the clutter, Tiffany's eyes were immediately drawn to the shoebox that had once contained her stash. Her legs came out from under her, causing her to sink to the floor. All her money was gone. All she could do was weep, so that was what she did.

"You still got me," a soothing voice said reassuringly.

"Huh?" Tiffany said, looking around the room for the source.

"You know I got you, girl," the calming voice said in its singsong manner.

She tilted her head and looked at her purse, puzzled at the voice emanating from within it. She snatched it open and checked her cell phone, but it wasn't on.

"Right here," the half-ounce of P.I.G.'s finest said, chuckling. "I'm here for you."

"I know you are," Tiffany sniffled, removing the drug and her shooter. For the next couple of hours, she made small talk with her crack as she smoked.

When she finally got around to surveying the damage, a pattern began to take shape. Wanda's stuff seemed to be tossed with care, while hers was destroyed, much of it missing. The clothes that weren't stolen were cut up, and there was urine on her bed.

"This bitch right here!" Tiffany said, shaking her head as she dialed her phone.

When Mike heard the distress in her voice, he dropped

what he was doing and rushed over. When he arrived, Tiffany was curled up on the sofa of the ransacked room. "Fuck happened here?" Mike asked, looking around the room.

"We…well, no, I got robbed," Tiffany replied with a pain-filled chuckle.

"Don't worry. Ima find out who did this," Mike boomed.

"Oh, I already know who did it," Tiffany replied.

"Who?" Mike demanded, sitting next to her on the sofa.

"Take a look around, then you tell me. It ain't hard to tell," she replied.

Mike didn't budge, looking at Tiffany, confused.

"Go on. Look around," Tiffany urged.

Moments later, Mike stormed back in the room, fuming. "That trifling lil bitch!" he yelled.

"Trifling ain't the word," Tiffany said. "Bitch peed in my bed!"

"What all she took? I'll get it back," Mike said in earnest.

"Uh, let's see…$15,000, my clothes, jewelry, shoes…" Tiffany went on. "My panties…"

Mike was dialing his phone was she spoke. "She gon' give it all back."

* * *

Wanda was in the middle of a long pull from her shooter when Mike's name appeared on her caller ID. She hit the ignore button, sending the call to voicemail. After holding the smoke for as long as humanly possible, Wanda exhaled. "Lemme see what dis nigga talking about," she said, checking her voicemail.

She knew Mike was gonna take Tiffany's word about the robbery, so she intended to avoid him for as long as she could. When she heard the message, she was filled with hope. *Perhaps there is a way out.* To be sure, she replayed it again.

"Babe, it's me. There was a break-in at the house. Are you okay? Call me and let me know you're okay," Mike said convincingly.

Wanda immediately returned the call and told Mike she was fine and on her way. She glared at P.I.G., daring him to complain about the ounce she was taking out of the house.

P.I.G. stared back but said nothing. The way she was hitting that pipe was victory enough for him. P.I.G. was a vet, and he knew the end was near.

"I'll see y'all later. My man need me," Wanda told her fellow crackheads before turning her nose up at P.I.G. again.

"I can't wait to see that black-hearted bitch fall," P.I.G. said once Earl closed the door behind her. One thing he knew was that no one could keep smoking at that rate and not fall. He had been taking note of the gradual increase of her purchases and consumption. He noticed the subtle changes in her appearance that most people would miss. The jeans and shirt were designer, though wrinkled. Her usually meticulously done hair was pulled back into a lazy ponytail, tucked under a Braves cap. P.I.G. knew the difference between a bad hair day and a woman's demise. He'd seen it hundreds of times, but none would be as sweet as Wanda's. Just her sticking around to smoke with the "commoners" spoke volumes. "Just a matter of time," P.I.G. snarled. "And I'll be waiting, broom in hand."

* * *

"Oh my God! What happened here?" Wanda exclaimed as she walked into the house.

"And the award for Best Actress goes to…" Tiffany chuckled at Wanda's weak performance.

"Bitch, sit you rotten ass down," Mike said in a deadly tone.

"Wh-what's going on, Mike? What's she talking 'bout?" Wanda said, obeying the command to sit. She looked back and forth between Tiffany and Mike, wearing a pained expression. When her eyes met Tiffany's, Tiffany sucked her teeth and looked away. "Fuck you sucking your teeth at me, bitch. I ain't take yo' damn money," Wanda yelled, rising to her feet.

"Sit yo' ass back down!" Mike ordered through clenched teeth. "And who said anything about her money?"

"I…I'm…I'm sayin' tho'…" Wanda stammered. Realizing she was caught, she decided to Rush Tiffany. Getting her ass kicked was inevitable, so at least she could get a piece of Tiffany first.

Mike was too quick for Wanda and intercepted her before she made it across the room and began to pummel her. He was hitting her with his fists, feet, knees, and elbows. The heavy blows sounded off in the small room.

Tiffany, being unaccustomed to violence, was absolutely terrified. "Stop it! You're gonna kill her!" she yelled, trying to pull Mike away.

In his fury, Mike wheeled around and slapped her across the room. The blow left her on the floor, dazed. "Babe? Are you okay?" Mike said, rushing to her side.

Tiffany was too stunned to reply. She watched Wanda spit blood and a tooth onto the carpet. Wanda took advantage of the reprieve and took off out the door.

Mike gave chase, but Wanda was too quick in running for her life. She was in her car and locking the door by the time

Mike made it through the door. He took the front steps in a single bound and was at the car before Wanda could back out.

Wanda slammed the car in reverse and stood on the gas pedal. The tires squealed as she pulled out and down the street. She made it, but she left behind all her worldly possessions, things she would never see again in life.

Back inside, Mike found Tiffany packing what was left of her belongings. "What are you doing, baby?" Mike asked when he found her loading her bags.

In an instant, she had become tired of the sex and violence – tired of the club and tired of being a prostitute. She wanted to go home and be Tiffany again. "I can't do this no more. I'm going home," she pleaded.

"Fuck you mean, 'home'?" Mike growled. "You belong to me!" he yelled, snatching her up.

"Nigga, you don't own me!" Tiffany yelled, determine to take control of her life.

Mike's hand was a blur as it sped toward her face. The slap, though not as hard, hurt more than the first because this one was deliberate. "Bitch, I DO own you. You are my property! Do you understand?" Mike screamed, inches from her face and clutching her harshly by the shoulders.

Tiffany was so scared she could only nod her head. She was shaking like a leaf, trying to pee on herself.

Mike sensed that he had accomplished his goal and softened his tone. "Look, baby…" he began, kissing her forehead as he spoke. "We are a team, you and me. I need you," he said, feeling her relax with his words. "Ima make sure you get all your money back and then some. After we reach our goal, it's over. You're coming to live with me. That's if you belong to me. Do you? Do you belong to me?" Mike then removed her clothes and laid her down as he spoke.

"Yes, I'm yours," Tiffany moaned as Mike entered her.

"Tell me you're my property," Mike demanded, stroking her firmly.

"Yes. Yes, I'm all yours!" Tiffany yelled as an orgasm shook her small frame.

CHAPTER 20

Mike had put out a $10,000 reward for whoever brought Wanda to him. He wanted her alive... so he could kill her himself. Her little stunt cost him fifteen stacks to replace the money she stole from Tiffany. It didn't matter that he drove Tiffany even harder and charged more for her services.

Once Wanda polished off the last of the ounce she got from P.I.G., she was back on the hunt, knowing full well that P.I.G. despised her and would turn her in on the strength, let alone ten stacks. That bridge was burned.

Word was out at most of the other smokehouses in town, further reducing her options. The few renegades who either had the balls or lacked the brains to trap on the street or out of hotel rooms had pure D bullshit, straight chalk.

Wanda was born again when she found the card Pony had given her months before at the bottom of her purse. She remembered a sample of that butta came with it.

Pony knew about the bounty on Wanda's head, but he wasn't interested in claiming it. At the same time, he wasn't messing with her either. His life was drama free, and he wanted to keep it that way. Instead, he directed her to the address of the small smokehouse he had set up for Marcus.

Wanda was thrilled to find out trick-ass Marcus had a package. As bad as he used to sweat her, she didn't intend to spend a dime. She knew the money she'd stolen from Tiffany wouldn't last. Even if Mike hadn't blackballed her from every club, who wanted a dancer missing a front tooth?

* * *

"Today is ya lucky day," she said, pulling in front of the small rental house Marcus operated out of. Another advantage to seducing Marcus was his shared hatred of both Mike and Tiffany. He could be an asset in her plans for revenge.

She had long ago copied the keys to Mike's condo and gleaned the combination to his safe. The only thing she lacked was the courage to hit the lick. Years back, Wanda had previously watched Mike beat a girl to death over some missing money—cash Wanda herself had stolen. She planned to make an anonymous tip once she got that money out of the safe.

It took several minutes of beating on the door for Wanda to revive Marcus from the coma-like sleep.

"Fuck! Beating on da do like da po-lice!" Marcus grumbled. Then, being the foolish, reckless junkie he was, he pulled the door open without even checking to make sure it wasn't the police.

"Hey, Mr. Man," Wanda said seductively, pushing past Marcus. She was relieved to see he was alone, and better yet, he hadn't begun to get high. One thing Wanda knew was that once a junkie started smoking for the day, he had no use for some pussy.

"What time is it?" Marcus inquired, blinking rapidly and trying to make sure his eyes weren't deceiving him. He couldn't believe Wanda was actually there and being nice to him.

"Oooh wee! Time to brush yo' teeth," Wanda said in jest as she looked around the spare room.

The room was empty except for a queen-sized mattress on the floor and a camcorder on a tripod facing the bed. Marcus obviously fancied himself a mini P.I.G.

"Whatcha tryina cop?" Marcus asked, flopping back on the mattress to go back to sleep.

"Nigga, you been sniffing my ass for a year, and now that I hand-delivered the coochie, you treat me like a customer," Wanda said, peeling off her clothes.

Marcus was now fully awake and grinning from ear to ear. "That's what's up!" he exclaimed, reaching to pull her onto the mattress.

"You gotta go slay that dragon first," Wanda teased.

Marcus was up in a flash to go brush his teeth.

While he was gone, Wanda picked up the shooter next to the bed and loaded it with a large chunk of crack from the plate on the table.

From the bathroom, even over the sound of running water, Marcus could hear the familiar and tempting sizzle of the drug being smoked. He didn't know what he wanted to hit first, the pipe or Wanda. He was rock hard thinking of both. Marcus stripped in record time and lunged on the bed. He tried to get in between her legs, but they snapped closed.

"You gotta kiss her and get her ready," Wanda purred.

Marcus snatched his grill out and dove between her thighs.

Wanda pulled her legs up from the back of her knees, putting herself in the buck. "Mmm...eat that pussy," Wanda said, preparing to fake an orgasm. To her surprise, Marcus licked and sucked her so well she came for real. "Come on and get you some of this wet-wet," she purred, pulling him up.

As soon as Marcus got inside her, he began humping wildly. "You like dis dick?" he demanded to know. "Tell me you like this dick!"

"Ooh, Daddy! You beating this pussy up," Wanda replied, trying her best not to laugh. At the rate he was going, he was going to blow his load before she got him to commit to her plans. When his breath grew ragged and his eyes began to roll into the back of his head, Wanda pushed him out of her. "Hold up. Lemme ride that big ol' dick," she said, causing him to grin at the compliment. When she slid down onto him, she began to whisper in his ear, "You gonna help me get some get-back?"

"Yeah! At who?" he asked, flailing his head from side to side as she rode him. At that moment, Marcus would have agreed to kill the Pope, the president, and whoever else she told him to.

"Mike. I want you to kill Mike," Wanda purred as she contracted her vaginal muscles.

It was too much for Marcus, and he let loose inside of her. "Don't worry. Ima kill dat fuck nigga first chance I get!" Marcus swore once he caught his breath.

"Well, Ima give you the chance and the keys to his condo," Wanda said, squeezing his rapidly deflating dick.

The couple then commenced to smoke the rest of the day away. Marcus actually turned his phone off, as he didn't plan on making any more sales that day.

It wouldn't be the first package he'd fucked up. Pony was giving him plenty of rope to hang himself, and Marcus was quickly tightening the noose.

CHAPTER 21

Fueled by Mike's promises of being together and living together, Tiffany was tricking like there was no tomorrow. She was servicing four to five men a day. Mike often told her he loved her and then sent her off to sell herself.

Her steadily increasing consumption of cocaine had her senses numb. In her drug-induced stupor, she pretended she was an actress. Each customer met a different persona, depending on their desires. There was the sweet, demure Tiffy, who was shy and innocent, almost virginal. Then there was Sasha, the stone-cold freak. Tiffany could read a man in seconds and would simply zone out and turn her body over to one of her alter-egos.

She was in such high demand that Mike split her earnings 50/50 and then raised her fee. With the money she earned, Tiffany was able to live the lifestyle she once only dreamed of. Tiffany now shopped at Lenox Mall and ate at the best restaurants.

In return, Tiffany never balked at anything Mike asked her to do. But then that day came.

"Oh, hell naw!" Tiffany yelled upon arrival at her "date's"

house. She whipped out her cell and called Mike, tapping her foot furiously as the phone rang. "I ain't about to do no porno!" she yelled into the phone as soon as Mike answered.

"This is the last one, baby! This is it!" Mike said gleefully. "We did it!"

"Did what?" Tiffany asked, getting caught up in his enthusiasm.

"The money they gonna pay us puts us where we need to be. It's over. Just me and you!" he said.

"So I ain't gotta dance or date no more?" Tiffany asked dubiously.

"No, no nothing. Just you and me, baby," Mike said soothingly, then threw in an "I love you" for good measure.

"So if I do this, I can move in now?" Tiffany asked wistfully.

"Baby, you can move in tomorrow!" Mike shot back. He was glad to be on the phone so Tiffany couldn't see the *"Yeah, right"* expression on his face.

"Look, do whatever them folks want you to do, then bring ya clothes over tomorrow," Mike said convincingly.

"You for real?" Tiffany asked, bouncing like a small child.

"Yeah, baby. Sure," he replied before saying his goodbyes.

"A'ight. Let's do this!" Tiffany yelled to the confused crew.

The director sprang into action and put her through every sexual scenario known. At his direction, Tiffany engaged in a lesbian scene with a white girl, and to her surprise, she actually enjoyed it. Then she was pummeled simultaneously by two black men.

Even when one of them eased into her rectum, she was busy mentally redecorating Mike's condo. She was so caught up in her own mind that she didn't even hear the director call, "Cut!" It seemed like only a few minutes, but in actuality, they compiled hours of material – footage that would eventually be published in movies, magazines, and on the Internet.

After showering the sweat and semen from her body, Tiffany went home to pack. She had turned her last trick, and tomorrow she would be moving in with her boo. For the night, all she planned to do was smoke.

* * *

The next afternoon, Tiffany was humming a happy tune as she stuffed her belongings into her bags. She was pleasantly surprised when she ran out of room in her luggage only halfway through her closet. She had replaced everything Wanda had stolen or destroyed and then some.

At the same time Tiffany was naively stuffing her clothes in her bags, Mike was across town stuffing himself inside of Peaches.

Peaches was a fine young thing Mike had bagged in the 'hood when he stopped for gas. Although he generally avoided the 'hood and hoodrats, Peaches was something to see—truly a sight to behold. Standing right at six feet tall, she caught his attention, but her round ass held it. Mike expected her to sweat him and/or his Porsche truck, but Peaches didn't give either a second glance. He started to push once the tank was full, but he couldn't. The girl was a knockout! Drop-dead gorgeous, she looked like a taller version of Ashanti, but her eyes were a pale shade of blue. Her breasts and ass were giving the fabric of her clothing all it could handle. To top it off, she was young—real young.

It took some of Mike's best game to get the girl in the car.

She told him she was eighteen, but her conversation told him sixteen, tops. He couldn't care less though. The younger, the better.

Mike wasted no time once he got her to the condo. There was no small talk, no blunts, and nothing to eat or drink. He rushed her into the bedroom and ran up in her. He was almost a foot deep inside of Peaches when his cell phone began to vibrate on the nightstand. "Shit!" he cursed, seeing Tiffany's name on the display.

"What's wrong?" Peaches inquired about the outburst.

"Nothing, shawty. Turn over!" Mike replied. He had been meaning to call Tiffany all day to "postpone" her move-in date. *Does dat bitch really expect to move in? To be my girl? After all the tricks and making a damn porno?* He almost laughed out loud at how gullible the girl was.

When Peaches obeyed his command to turn over and stuck her perfect ass high in the air, thoughts of Tiffany and her problem vanished. He contemplated what to do with Peaches as he slammed in and out of her. Mike was far from a tender dick, but damn! *If you a pimp, then pimp, nigga*, he scolded himself. He decided to keep her for a minute and then put her to work. *P.I.M.P.*

* * *

Marcus rechecked the pistol as he pressed his ear to Mike's front door. He couldn't hear anything through the heavy oak, so he pressed on cautiously. He'd seen Mike rush the young girl inside a few minutes earlier, and judging by the look in his eye, he assumed he was up in her by now. He slid the key into the lock, then waited another minute to turn it. It took another full minute before he went past the point of no return and turned the doorknob.

Marcus rushed in with his gun eye high, ready to murder something. The front room was empty, but the sound of vigorous sex could be heard coming from the back. He stealthily followed the noise until he was standing in the open doorway of Mike's bedroom.

Mike was hitting her so well that Marcus almost hated to interrupt. He had Peaches flat on her stomach, pounder her from behind. Marcus could hear her coochie splashing from across the room.

The initial plan was to pistol-whip Mike and talk some shit like they do in the movies or one of those corny "black author" books. Instead, he raised the large gun and shot Mike in the back, just like a coward would do.

Mike went limp instantly as the heavy forty-five-caliber slug tore through his spine.

Peaches hesitated in confusion, then screamed in horror when she realized what was happening.

"Shut up! Shut the fuck up!" Marcus pleaded desperately, as if her screams would alert the neighbors more than the sound of gunfire.

When Peaches next opened her mouth to scream again, a bullet sped into it and out the back of her young head. Mike was still squirming, so Marcus put a bullet in the back of his head as well.

Marcus, being a petty thief at heart, stole a roll of cash and some jewelry that was lying around. "You mind if I get this?" Marcus asked sarcastically, picking up a bottle of Cognac. "'Preciate it." He chuckled when Mike didn't answer. He stuffed his pockets with loot and made his escape.

Of course he knew nothing of the safe nor its contents. Wanda planned to come back and clean that out on her own.

In an odd twist of fate, Tiffany pulled directly into the parking space as Marcus pulled out. Each was too consumed by their thoughts to notice the other. She had been dialing Mike's number since leaving home and never got an answer. "I know he here," she said aloud, noticing the Porsche and Lexus both in their places.

As she grabbed a couple of the smaller bags, a police car whipped up and stopped at the building entrance. Two officers jumped out urgently and trotted inside. Tiffany followed behind and waited on the next elevator. The next car came, and Tiffany rode up to Mike's floor. When she arrived, she could see Mike's door was wide open, and she tilted her head curiously at the anomaly.

As she neared, the younger of the two police who had rushed in rushed out and tossed his cookies in the hallway.

"What happened? What's wrong?" Tiffany asked the officer, who was now turning green. He was too busy regurgitating donuts to respond.

Tiffany left the sick man and rushed into the apartment. The front room was in order, so she followed the sound of the second officer's radio and found him standing over the splattered bodies. A bloodcurdling scream alerted the police officer to Tiffany's presence, but before he could say a word, she fainted.

When Tiffany came to, she found herself on the living room sofa with an EMS tech hovering over her. For the next few minutes, she watched the detectives and CSI personnel swarming in and out of the condo. When she regained her composure, she was taken to the Major Crimes Department at police headquarters. There, she was grilled by the detectives assigned to the case.

"What was your relationship to the decedent?" the older

of the two asked genially.

"To who?" Tiffany asked, confused by the new term.

"The dead guy," the other cop shot back. "How did you know the dead guy?"

"Oh, Mike? He was my boyfriend." Tiffany sobbed. "We were moving in together today."

Her answer caused the detectives to share a conspiratorial glance. The two cops excused themselves to huddle in the hallway.

The next person to enter the room was a CSI tech who swabbed Tiffany's hands for gunshot reside. She had become a suspect.

For the next several hours, she fielded hundreds of questions. "Who was the girl? Did Mike have enemies? Where did he get the $200,000 in the safe?"

Tiffany couldn't answer any of their questions. The reality of there being a woman present shook her soul. When the GSR test came back negative, she was cleared.

"If it wasn't for your loss, we'd have called Dekalb County. They got a warrant for your arrest," the portly cop told her.

"Thank you," Tiffany mumbled, grateful not to be going to jail, especially with the half-ounce of crack in her purse. Since she was too shaken up to drive, a patrol car took her home. She decided she could retrieve her car in the morning; for now she just needed a blast.

* * *

The next morning, a federal investigation was set off by the money found in the safe. In a week's time, the club, the houses, and the cars were seized by the Feds.

Tiffany was out of a job and a place to live overnight, instantly jobless and homeless. The only thing that remained was a serious drug habit that demanded to be fed.

CHAPTER 22

Wanda was pissed at not being able to get at Mike's fortune, but his being dead was the next best thing. Since Marcus was still getting good dope from Pony, she slid under him.

Pony was still looking out for his childhood friend by giving him ounces to "sell." He was supposed to bring back $500 on each one, but he never did. Pony only did it to keep Marcus out of his hair. He was getting rich and didn't need the distractions Marcus was sure to bring.

Marcus and Wanda smoked far more than they sold. There was always some sort of P.I.G.-style freak show going on at the house. He and Wanda had sex with each other and whoever else happened by.

Pony was feeding him with a long-handled spoon but was growing tired of him. Marcus was hanging on by a thread but didn't even know it.

* * *

Pony heard through the grapevine that Tiffany was dancing at Dimes on Buford Highway. Dimes was a questionable strip club that featured black, white, and Mexican girls. The local police made arrests for prostitution or drugs there on a regular basis.

Tiffany, with her outrageous masturbation show, was an instant hit. Once the regulars from Club Chocolate found out where she was, they flocked to see her, boosting her status with the owner. She was making plenty of money to support her addiction without having to trick. Each night after work, she'd pick up a package from P.I.G. and retire to the extended-stay hotel she called home.

"Hey, stranger!" Tiffany said, delighted to see the familiar face, known to have the best dope in town.

"Hey, yourself. I've been looking for you," Pony said, extending his arms for a hug.

"Well, you found me," Tiffany said, accepting the hug. "Wow! I see you missed me," she teased, feeling an erection rise instantly in his pants.

"Come on. Let's get outta here," Pony said, his voice hoarse with desire.

"I can't go yet. I ain't made my rent yet," she whined, stripper talk for *"Sure, we can go fuck, but you gotta pay me."*

"Shit, shawty, you ain't got to worry 'bout rent or nothing else, long as you wit' me," Pony bragged, backing up enough so she could see he was balling.

Tiffany could tell by Pony's treatment of her that he expected the old, sweet, naïve Tiffany, so she became her. She contracted her vaginal muscles so tight that Pony wondered if she wasn't a virgin.

He lasted about two minutes before slumping over, head-over-heels in love with her. "Do you know how long I wanted to do that to you?" Pony asked between gulps of air.

"Yeah," Tiffany said with a giggle, going into little girl

mode.

"What you mean, 'yeah'?" Pony said, chuckling and tickling her sides.

Tiffany laughed and squirmed, not because she was actually ticklish, but because "Whatever the customer wants" was her mantra. "I always knew you liked me. I liked you too," she said coyly. "If I wasn't with Marcus—"

"That nigga is a fool! You with me now," he said confidently, then filled her in on Marcus's latest antics.

"I hope you don't mind," Tiffany asked as she fished her shooter out of her purse.

"I do mind," Pony said bluntly. He was shocked to see she was now smoking out of a pipe. "It's time to let that shit go!" he said.

"But, baybeee, I like to get high!" Tiffany whined.

Pony pondered in silence for a moment. He had wanted Tiffany since third grade. He waited until he got his weight up before even stepping to her. He figured she was still using, just not actually in the pipe. "Take that shit in the bathroom," he barked. "If you gon' be wit' me, that shit gotta go!"

"Thank you, Daddy! Ima quit," Tiffany squealed, although she had already made up her mind to bounce if he didn't let her smoke. "Wait till you see how horny it make me," she added over her shoulder as she rushed into the bathroom.

Pony's eyes were glued to her lovely ass as she bounced away. Crack or no crack, he was sprung.

As Tiffany twisted and turned her pipe under the flame, she plotted on how to deal with her new man. The ideal situation was to get him smoking again. Since he was plugged in with P.I.G. and that good dope, they could get high all day. She got a good laugh out of picturing herself as Pony's Blast, only prettier. If that didn't work, she resolved that she would ride the Pony Express as long as she could. "No way I'm letting you go," she said to a piece of cocaine before smoking it. Once she finished her package, she went back into the bedroom and sucked Pony's brains out through his dick, sealing the deal, she hoped.

* * *

After her attempts to get Pony back on the pipe failed, Tiffany went back to dancing. This allowed her both the money and the time away to get high. Pony kept on her about her drug use, so she hid it from him. At the club, she could smoke as much as she liked, but she also stole a blast or two at home when she could. If Pony was careless enough to leave any drugs unattended, they were smoked.

Almost all the girls at the club were on something. It was a common sight to see someone snorting, smoking, shooting, or popping something. The savvy manager got a cut from the select dealers she allowed to operate inside of the establishment. A skinny, tattooed white boy named Two handled the meth, while a Mexican called Droopy had the weed. There was a smooth black dude who called himself Ali-Rock who had the blow, hard or soft.

All the dealers had *carte blanche* throughout the club and unlimited access to the private rooms. It wasn't unusual for them to sometimes trade their wares for sexual favors.

Ali-Rock had taken a liking to the back of Tiffany's throat, and they bartered daily. It was during one of those bartering sessions that Pony decided to stop by and see his "wifey."

When Pony stepped into the club, he was greeted by a tiny Asian girl with huge breasts. "Hey, you looking for your girl?" she asked mischievously.

"Excuse me?" Pony said, startled by both the question and the size of her breasts.

"You're Pony, right? Tiffy's man?" she said, drawing his attention back to her face. Like most of the other girls, Angel hated Tiffany. She had been the star attraction until Tiffany came along, playing with herself. Her outrageous masturbation show stole the show.

"Um, yeah…where she at?" Pony said, scanning the stages.

"Follow me," Angel said, leading him by the arm. She led him into the private room that Tiffany and Ali-Rock had just excused her from. When they arrived, Angel pushed the door open and stepped aside.

"Uh huh! Suck that dick, you nasty bitch!" Ali-Rock demanded as Tiffany worked her head furiously. She was ass naked in full slut mode, the way Ali-Rock liked her. Tiffany was literally gagging herself trying to please him.

"Hey, Tiffy, ya man's here," Angel sang before walking off.

Pony stood there in shock, unable to move or speak. If the music hadn't been so loud, they all could have heard his heart break.

When Tiffany looked up from Ali-Rock's throbbing crotch, she was so surprised that she tried to speak before removing his dick from her throat. The resulting gargling, gagging sound caused Ali-Rock to crack up laughing. "Ayo, ma, don't talk with your mouth full."

As he laughed, Pony turned his head to leave.

"Hold up, yo! It's not what it looks like!" Ali-Rock laughed again, adding insult to injury. His laughter reverberated in Pony's ears as he left.

Tiffany, knowing full well what a burnt bridge looked

like, kept on bobbing her weave.

A single tear escaped Pony's eye as he climbed back into his truck. In truth, he knew he could only blame himself. He had broken the cardinal rule: You can't turn a ho into a housewife. It was his bad, and he knew it.

CHAPTER 23

Marcus and Wanda finished polishing off an ounce, not even a full twenty-four hours after receiving it. He was expected to pay $500 for every ounce Pony fronted him. Marcus always came up short, but this time he didn't even sell one crumb. They tricked off with some and smoked the rest. "Ain't the first package I fucked up." Marcus laughed. The way he figured it, Pony owed him; they were partners. It was his lick that got them started, and he was the one who had put him on with P.I.G. Last but not least, he knew Tiffany had moved in with Pony months earlier and hadn't tripped about it. With all that in mind, he dialed Pony's number.

Pony was in a foul mood after just seeing the love of his life with some dude's cock in her mouth. He was busy putting her belongings (minus what he'd bought her) by the curb. He was tearing up pictures, trying not to cry, when his phone rang. His first thought was to ignore the call, thinking it was Tiffany with some lame excuse like *"Baby, I don't know how his dick got in my mouth."* Still, Pony picked up the phone, eager to hear whatever she had to say. He hoped and prayed he had somehow misunderstood what he saw.

Damn, he coulda been raping my girl! his pussy-whipped mind screamed. "This nigga here," Pony fumed when he saw Marcus's name on the ID screen. He was eager to vent his frustration on someone, so he took the call. "Yeah?" Pony barked.

"What's good, play?" Marcus sang playfully. "I need to get witcha."

"You got my money for the last one? Ain't shit if you ain't got my money," Pony shot back.

"Money?" Marcus chuckled. "I know you ain't trippin' 'bout no money." He actually pulled the phone back to look at it and make sure he had the right number. He couldn't believe his ace from the first place was fronting on him.

"Nigga, I sell blow. I can't come up giving you all my work!" Pony yelled.

"What you tripping on?" Marcus whined.

The pleading in his voice caused Wanda to take notice.

"Trippin'!? You junkie-ass nigga! I got ya tripping!" Pony shouted. He was feeling better with every insult he hurled at his former friend. "Get my money up, fuck nigga!" he said, taking it too far.

Marcus looked at his phone again, hearing the game-changing insult. He knew he was a junkie, but a fuck nigga? *Dem's fighting words,* he thought. "'Fuck nigga'?" Marcus asked, daring Pony to say it again.

"Yeah, fuck nigga! Bitch nigga, ho nigga, dick-in-the-booty-ass nigga!" Pony yelled.

There was a deadly silence on the line as Marcus digested what he heard. The insults had awakened the murderous demons in his head. They had been subdued by the mind-numbing amount of drugs Marcus had been consuming, as well as his offing of Mike and the ho he was fucking, but now that the pipeline had been cut off, they were stirring.

"Hello? You there?" Pony asked when no reply came.

"Yeah, I'm here. I'll be to see you," Marcus said in a dangerous tone before hanging up.

It was at that moment that Pony realized he'd gone too far. He knew firsthand that Marcus was a killer. He wasn't someone who just marked a nigga; he was an actual killer. There was a difference.

Pony knew his life would be over if he didn't act fast. His first call went to the Homicide Unit, where he anonymously dropped a dime about Mike's murder.

The next call was one he'd been contemplating for months, and now the time was ripe for it. "Say, shawty. Dis Pony. I know who kilt y'all daddy," Pony told one of Red's still-grieving sons. With that one phone call, Pony killed Marcus without busing a shot, and he made up a scenario to excluded his own role in the crime. He finished the call with the address where Marcus could be found.

Pony's next call went to Jasmine, seeking refuge in the back of her throat—not to mention he needed someone there to give him strength if Tiffany came home.

* * *

Wanda was able to glean from Marcus's side of the conversation that he'd blown his connect. She still had most of the money she had stolen from Tiffany, but she had no intention of supporting both of their habits. It had been a great ride, but the Marcus train was at the end of the line. It was time to move on.

She convinced Marcus to sit tight while she made a run to P.I.G.'s to cop. She even wrote down his order for a supreme fish sandwich before she left.

Wanda pulled on Tiffany's Coogi dress that now fit like a glove due to her weight loss and pushed off to the next chapter in the drama that was her life.

* * *

It was well after midnight when Marcus finally accepted the fat that Wanda was not coming back. She had turned off her phone, and according to the regulars at P.I.G.'s, she had come and gone hours earlier. "Bitch ain't even bring me my fish sandwich!" Marcus fumed as he tucked his pistol into his waistband. He intended to go make some collections on some of the credit he'd been doling out over the last few months.

His luck was still holding up as two of Red's sons kicked in the front door only minutes after he left. He drove around town, pulling his gun on people he knew and taking whatever money or drugs they had. Finally, once his hate was boiling, he headed to settle a score.

It was just past three in the morning when Marcus pulled in front of Pony's condo. He sat there for a while smoking the cocaine he'd robbed from some kid at a gas station. "Fuckin' garbage!" he exclaimed as he exhaled the low-quality dope. "I'm smoking dis bullshit while dat fuck nigga got dat glass!" he growled, further amping himself up. He mentally whipped himself into a frenzy, then headed up the stairs.

The noise of the front door being kicked in woke Pony and Jasmine from their slumber, but Marcus was in the room before they could react. "What it do?" Marcus asked with a devilish smile.

"Shawty, what the hell you doing?" Pony asked, noticing

the gun in Marcus's hand.

"Don't ack like you don't know," Marcus shot back. "Fuck nigga."

"Man, I know you ain't tripping 'bout that shit!" Pony laughed nervously.

"Um, excuse me, fellas…" Jasmine said, getting out of the bed. "I'm finna go so y'all can handle y'all bizness," she said, bending over to pick her panties off the floor.

The sight of Jasmine's naked ass caused Marcus to pause.

Pony took advantage of the distraction and reached for the nine-millimeter pistol on his nightstand. He didn't make it. A well-placed shot put his brains on the headboard as he went to meet his maker.

Jasmine, being the hoodrat she was, was no stranger to violence. She fully understood that the next words out of her mouth meant the difference between life and death. "Come on, pimp. Lemme show you where the stash at," she said, dropping the panties back on the floor. She was grateful that Pony liked to show off his goods. Actually, she had planned to send some of the goons from her projects to rob him anyway. "You gon' hafta break me off tho'," Jasmine said as she led Marcus to another room.

"Oh, Ima break you off a'ight," he replied, getting an erection from her swagger.

When Jasmine heard the lust in his voice, she knew she was out of the woods. "I ain't stingy with the pussy." She chuckled. "So don't be stingy with the dope."

"Fuck!" Marcus gasped as he entered a room where several kilos sat in various stages of preparation. He knew Pony was getting to the money, but he didn't know he was doing it like that. "And dis nigga spoon-feeding me onions!"

he said as he loaded up the dope.

"Don't forget about me," Jasmine reminded as he put it in the bag.

He started to say something fly, but the sarcastic remark disappeared into thin air when he turned back to Jasmine. She was spread eagle on the ground, fingering herself. Two minutes later, he was on his way out of the house with the dope, minus the couple of ounces he threw Jasmine. She put it on him so well that he left without any of the money.

As soon as Marcus left, Jasmine went about the task of removing all traces of herself ever being there. She wiped down every surface from everything she ever touched. Next, she pulled the pillowcase containing her DNA off the bed. It was a lot of work, but the $130 she left with was compensation.

By the time Tiffany pulled up, the trash collector had come and gone with her belongings that Pony had set on the curb. An anonymous call had the complex swarming with police. Tiffany joined the crowd of curious onlookers just in time to watch Pony being removed in a body bag.

CHAPTER 24

As Wanda sat in the lobby of the free clinic, her emotions ran the gamut. She vacillated between wanting to cry and wanting to laugh. "I know I am not pregnant." She chuckled. "Probably got the flu or something." It had been months since she had her last period, but it was the nagging flu symptoms that had sent her to the clinic.

Wanda had been selling her body one way or another since she was thirteen and had never gotten pregnant. Now she was twenty-nine, and she certainly didn't think it possible. She and Marcus had been having unprotected sex for months, not to mention all the guys she'd tricked with or without him.

If I am pregnant, Ima slide right back in there, she thought enthusiastically at the prospect of hooking back up with Marcus. Word on the street had him doing it real big lately.

When Marcus killed Pony, he absorbed a little of his personality and began selling some of the blow instead of smoking it all. He was able to recoup from P.I.G. and keep it going…for now.

Wanda laid her head back in the chair in hopes of getting a little rest. Being banned from all the clubs and cut off from her gravy train, she had to go hard with the sex game to support herself. She had lost quite a bit of weight but was still fine, and the head was the stuff of legend.

Just as she drifted off to sleep, she heard her name being called. She looked up to see a pretty young nursing assistant scanning the room, repeating her name.

A twinge of regret overcame Wanda as she watched the young woman. She reminisced as to what could have been. She had once aspired to be a nurse when she grew up. However, she traded her future for boys and drugs before she had the chance to grow up.

"Wanda Creedmore?" the assistant called again, breaking Wanda from her spell just as the tears came.

"Right here, lil mama!" Wanda said, raising a hand. She got up and followed the girl into an examination room and took a seat.

"You can change into this. The doctor will be in, in a minute," the assistant said sweetly while handing Wanda a gown.

"Ms. Creedmore?" the doctor said when he walked in. He appeared to be as young as the assistant.

"Yeah, that's me," Wanda said, hoarse from having been asleep. A glance at the clock told her it had been almost two hours since the nurse took her blood and urine sample. Wanda was instantly antsy at the realization that she had been there so long without a blast. "Say, Doc, lemme get a quick smoke," she said, visualizing the large rock in her car.

"Huh?" the doctor questioned the strange request. He flashed a brilliant smile as he spoke, which made Wanda change her mind.

"Nothing, honey. I'm cool," she said flirtatiously.

The doctor's smile turned into a grimace as he read the results fro the battery of tests she had undergone. "How long have you had, uh…the flu?" the doctor asked without looking up.

"Off and on for a couple months. Probably that bird flu or whatever y'all got going 'round," she replied with a chuckle.

"Aches, pains, night sweats?" the doctor asked as he scribbled.

"Mmhmm," Wanda replied, searching his worried face for answers.

"Ma'am…" the doctor began, then paused. He had given the same grim news more than he thought possible, yet it never got any easier. "You have several sexually transmitted diseases," he said grimly, still avoiding eye contact.

"It ain't the end of the world, Doc. I've been burned before," Wanda interrupted. Her embarrassment caused her to cop an attitude. "Just gimme my shot so I can be up out dis bitch," she shot.

"Well…um…I'm afraid it's not as simple as that. While we can treat you for the gonorrhea and Chlamydia, there is, uh…well…there is no cure for the HIV virus," the doctor said, struggling with the deadly diagnosis.

"You saying I got HIV!?" Wanda demanded.

"No, ma'am. Judging by your T-cell count, you have full-blown AIDS, I'm afraid," he said, finally making eye contact. He went on to explain various treatment options and resources that were available, but Wanda didn't hear any of it. The last words she heard were "full-blown AIDS."

Wanda floated back to her car in a daze, clutching a handful of brochures and pamphlets that were given to her by the doctor. Once inside her car, she fished out her shooter and loaded a huge hit on the top. Wanda inhaled furiously, secretly hoping to stop her heart. When the first one didn't do the trick, she tried another, followed by another. She sat there in full view of anyone who happened by, smoking cocaine. It wasn't until the clinic rent-a-cop threatened to call the real police that she moved on.

* * *

The same way a cut doesn't hurt until you see the blood, Wanda went downhill quickly, knowing that she was sick—that she was dying. The only thing that gave her solace were the drugs. With her money gone, she sold her car to support her habit.

Wanda's only possessions were the dirty Coogi dress and a raggedy twenty-five caliber pistol that had gotten her laughed out of every pawnshop she tried to sell it in.

She knew she shouldn't be tricking with the deadly disease, but she had burned through the few ounces at an incredible rate. With no other options or resources available to her, she hit the ho stroll, along with the other streetwalkers. Steward Avenue was Atlanta's premier prostitution track. The name had been changed to Metropolitan Parkway in a failed attempt to clean up the area, but for those who bought or sold pussy, it would forever be Steward Avenue.

* * *

Tiffany had begun her downward spiral as well. After Mike's upscale club closed and she'd burned her bridges at Dimes, she found herself dancing in a sexy club on Steward Avenue.

She was living in a rundown motel near the club so she could be close to the action. Her life was out of control, but she was powerless to stop it.

Cocaine had totally claimed her soul. She danced, tricked, and occasionally stole to get high. Every night, she swore it would be her last, but every morning, the vicious cycle repeated itself.

One morning, she headed home and made it only as far as her driveway. She couldn't get out of the car. She sat there staring at the house until the demons demanded that she leave.

When Tiffany pulled up at work, she cursed at the heavy police presence. "Oh shit! What now!?" she lamented as girl after girl was carted out in cuffs. Upset by the loss of easy income, but grateful to have missed whatever went down, Tiffany pulled off. For once, her tardiness had paid off.

None of her usual tricks were available, so she was penniless as she headed to P.I.G.'s. She dreaded what might be in store for her. By now, she had witnessed every sex act known to man and P.I.G.

When Tiffany told P.I.G. that she didn't have any money but had just come to watch a show and hang out, he knew it was time to push the issue. "Well, ain't no show tonight," P.I.G. said to the relief of Dondi, who was still sore from the show he'd just done with the Omen. "Tell you what..." P.I.G. said, grabbing his camera. "Lemme see this show you got that I've been hearing so much about."

Tiffany was so grateful that she wouldn't have to do anything more than masturbate. She instantly spread her legs and went at it.

The room was enveloped in silence as Tiffany worked her fingers. The only sounds to be heard were her moans and P.I.G.'s heavy breathing. He was drooling down the front of his shirt as he filmed the episode.

P.I.G. called for Blast so he could get a blow job while he

watched. Blast came out and sucked her teeth at Tiffany, then headed back to her room. As it turned out, he really didn't need her, because when Tiffany came, P.I.G. did too.

"Just about there," P.I.G. surmised as he watched Tiffany suck her earnings through her shooter. "Almost ripe," he said, feeling another erection growing at the thought.

"I gotta go," Tiffany announced, wrapping up her shooter and drugs. She had smoked just enough to quiet the monkey on her back. The rest, she intended to smoke in the solitude of her room.

"Okay, lil mama," P.I.G. said warmly. "We gotta do this again soon."

"That's what's up," Tiffany mumbled on her way out the door.

* * *

As soon as she left, P.I.G. forced Blast to blow him as he replayed the footage of Tiffany masturbating. Even though he was deep in his wife's throat, P.I.G. took the call on his vibrating phone. After all, business was business. "Yeah?" P.I.G. barked into the phone after checking the ID screen.

"'Bout to come shop witcha," Marcus said enthusiastically.

P.I.G. could hear his mouth twitching through the line. "Come on!" P.I.G. replied and flipped the phone closed. Like everyone, P.I.G. assumed Marcus was at least involved in Pony's murder. All of the sudden, he was selling ounces and buying half-kilos. He also knew there was a $10,000 bounty on Marcus's head. P.I.G. was waiting until Marcus fucked up all his money before turning him in. Since his re-ups were steadily declining from half-kilos to the couple of ounces he was now coming for, it was almost time to claim the reward. *Timing is everything*, P.I.G. mused as he let go in his wife's mouth.

CHAPTER 25

Mrs. Williams felt her heart literally stop as she watched two sheriff's deputies approach her door. "Will!" she yelled out, summoning her husband.

Hearing the distress in his wife's voice, Tiffany's father bolted from the den to her aid. "What's wrong?" he asked urgently when he reached her side.

Far too rattled for words, Mrs. Williams could only point toward the front door just as the officers reached it.

"Is this about my daughter?" Mr. Williams asked plainly as his wife held her breath, expecting the worst but praying for the best. It had been almost a year since Tiffany had left home, and they hadn't heard a word from her since.

"Sir, we are here with an arrest warrant for a Tiffany Williams, for failure to appear," the younger of the two deputies announced. The two deputies were polar opposites: one young, white, and overzealous; and the other an older, laidback black man.

Mrs. Williams finally exhaled as her husband explained that their daughter no longer lived there.

"We have not seen or heard from her in months," Mr.

Williams said strictly.

"We will need to have a look around to confirm that Tiffany Williams is not in the residence," the young, red-faced deputy said sternly. He was neither moved nor concerned with the pained expression on the couple's faces.

"Um, actually that won't be necessary," the older deputy interjected, looking at his partner as he spoke. "Have her turn herself over to the jail or give us a call if she comes home," he said, handing Mr. Williams a business card.

When the Williamses agreed to do one or the other, the deputies left to head to their car. They exchanged a terse glance that signaled an impending discussion on proper protocol.

Carlos had seen the sheriffs pull up and watched curiously from his window. When he saw them turn from the door, he went down to investigate. "Is everything okay over here?" he asked, making his way across the street. He hadn't seen Tiffany since that night at the club but had been hearing all kinds of rumors.

"And you are?" the gung-ho young cop asked, reaching for his pad.

"I'm a friend of the family," Carlos told the older deputy. "Is Tiffany okay?"

"That's what we are trying to find out," the black officer replied. "Do you know where we might locate her?"

Carlos's hesitation was obvious to the veteran deputy. He was clearly reluctant to deal with law enforcement on any level.

"Please. If you have any information, you need to be forthcoming. We want to help the girl," the young officer said with sentiment his partner didn't know he was capable of.

"Dimes," Carlos said loudly. "I heard she's dancing at

Dimes."

After writing down the information, the officer thanked Carlos for his cooperation and left. Armed with this new lead, they set off across town to scour the strip clubs.

* * *

Tiffany awoke in a strange bed with a stranger behind her. She scanned the room in an attempt to figure out where she was and with whom. It took several minutes for a few of the details that led her to the strange man's bed to come back.

Remembering that she had agreed to $300 to spend the night, she quietly checked her purse. After counting the three new $100 bills, she began looking for her panties.

"Oww!" Tiffany winced from pain as she sat down. "Nasty bastard." She frowned as the source of the pain came to mind. It was beyond her why some men wanted anal sex with a vagina an inch away. She tried to get dressed and leave, but her stirring woke the sleeping man.

"Mawnin'," he said in a heavy Southern drawl.

A wave of shame swept over Tiffany as a view of the man's face brought back more memories of the night she'd spent with him. He had definitely gotten his money's worth... and then some. "Hey," Tiffany replied, still rushing to dress. "Thank you for last night. I gotta go."

"Hol' up for a sec', lil mama," said the man, who looked to be the same age as her parents. He pulled back the sheets to reveal his morning erection.

"I gotta go!" Tiffany whined. She had enough money to get high for the day and definitely enough of this freak.

The man reached in his wallet and produced two more crisp $100 bills.

An hour later, she emerged from the hotel room with $500 and a serious pain in the ass. "Nasty bastard!" Tiffany cursed as she sat in her car.

* * *

Again, she thought about going home. But again, the monkey on her back demanded to be fed.

As she wrestled with the conflicting emotions, she watched curiously as an emaciated crackhead scurried away from P.I.G.'s house. "A knit dress in this heat?" Tiffany said, incredulous. It wasn't until the junkie made a sideways glance before darting into traffic that she realized the horrid sight was her one-time friend and roommate and mentor, Wanda. The only thing in worse shape than Wanda herself was the Coogi dress she wore.

The enmity and malice Tiffany harbored toward the woman vanished in an instant. In that same instant, Tiffany saw what lay ahead of her on her own path if she didn't pull it together. "What the hell am I doing?" she asked her reflection in the rearview mirror. She now noticed the changes in her appearance that she had ignored for months. "I'm going home!" Tiffany said adamantly. "Ima get me a few blasts, then I'm going home," she said, her resolve vanishing.

When Tiffany walked into P.I.G.'s place, she was greeted by the usual suspects. They were all glued to the plasma screen, laughing as they smoked. She returned their greeting, then turned to see what had everyone so captivated. They were watching the just-shot footage of Wanda performing oral sex on everyone in the room, including the women. P.I.G. could be heard barking lewd orders that were immediately carried out. Wanda had the expressionless face of someone already dead. Her ribs and vertebrae could be counted through her ashy skin.

Tiffany felt the urge to drop everything and run home, but the urge to stay was stronger.

"You wanna be a star too?" P.I.G. asked with a chuckle.

"Excuse me!?" the old Tiffany asked, unsure if she had heard the fat man correctly. "You'll never make me go out bad like that, you fat piece of shit!" she yelled as she approached him.

P.I.G. looked toward Earl for help, but Earl just turned his head.

If Tiffany had wanted to harm the man, she could have. Instead, she pummeled him verbally until her anger abated.

All of the occupants were in shock, knowing it was the kinda talk that got somebody either banned or degraded, the exact kind of insolence that had Wanda crawling on the floor performing for crumbs on the large screen that everyone was laughing at.

"Take it easy, sweetheart," P.I.G. said, raising his hands in mock surrender. "I was just joking." His fear calmed as Tiffany did. "Blast, make sure you hook our girl up," P.I.G. ordered as Tiffany took a seat.

Blast had a disgruntled air about her, sucking her teeth loudly as she set out to carry out her task. While she was gone, Tiffany saw the cause of her dismay. There Blast was on the screen with Wanda's head stuck between her legs as P.I.G. barked sickening orders.

When Blast returned, she pressed the package into Tiffany's hand and gave a discreet wink.

Tiffany glanced curiously into her hand and saw that Blast had slipped her an ounce instead of the eight ball she'd paid for. She quickly closed her hand, praying no one caught the exchange. They didn't; they were too engrossed in Wanda, now blowing a reluctant Earl on the screen. Tiffany stood up and made her way to the door without bothering to seek permission.

Earl said nothing about the breach of protocol and opened the door for her.

When Tiffany sat in her car and stared at the large amount of dope, she swore it would be her last. The hotel room was paid up for a couple of days, and with that much crack, she wouldn't have much use for food. The plan was simple: get high and then go home. But as was par for the course, when the drugs were gone, so was the plan.

CHAPTER 26

"**G**urrl, the po-lice was by here looking for you!" a dark-skinned Hispanic dancer announced to Tiffany as soon as she walked in the club.

"For me? For what?" Tiffany frowned, scanning her frazzled memory for a reason the police would be looking for her.

Before Sangria could make up a reason she thought the police were hunting her, the club manager appeared. "Come with me," the large woman said, wagging a thick finger.

Tiffany ran through a variety of excuses as they walked, but try as she did, she couldn't come up with a good lie, as she had no clue what they wanted with her.

"Have a seat, dear," the manager directed, taking a seat behind her desk.

"There must be some kinda misunderstanding," Tiffany said, figuring that would cover a range of scenarios.

"Look, I don't know why the cops are looking for you, and I don't care," the manager began.

Tiffany started to say something but was cut off by a wave of the woman's chubby hand.

"They been here every day for the last few days, but of course you wouldn't know that," the manager said.

Tiffany tried to speak again, but again she was silenced by the puffy hand.

"You know I can't have the folks in here like that. It's bad for business. Once you handle your business, you can come back," she said plainly.

"Well, whatcha gon' do now?" Tiffany questioned herself as she walked back to her car. She'd smoked the last of the dope Blast gave her that morning. The rent was due, and she was dead broke. To top it all off, that monkey on her back would be squealing soon, demanding to be fed. It was beginning to stir already.

Tiffany pulled out on Metropolitan but had to slam on the brakes to avoid being hit by a car that cut across all lanes of traffic. "Where the fuck are you tryina go!?" she yelled as the reckless driver pulled a dangerous U-turn.

The driver pulled up to a skinny prostitute just before another car could. The woman jumped in, and the driver pulled off as carelessly as he'd pulled up. The second driver pounded his wheel, frustrated at missing out.

As distasteful as it was, Tiffany now knew where her next buck was coming from. It beat her first thought, which was to go perform for P.I.G. and his camera. The thought of Wanda crawling around on the floor unnerved her. She knew if she kept asking P.I.G. for handouts, he would try her too. In her drug-induced reasoning, turning tricks would allow her to keep her dignity. There would be no roomful of people, no camera, and no P.I.G.

Tiffany stood out among the skinny crack whores on the block. She only stood on the block for thirty seconds before a car came to a screeching halt in front of her. Once it was parked, it took her less than a minute relieve the middle-aged white man of his tension and money. She got out of the car, simultaneously spitting his semen on the ground and stuffing his money in her bra. "Not bad for a couple minutes' work," Tiffany said with a chuckle as she hit the block again.

In a couple of hours, she decided to close up shop with a little over $600 for her efforts. She wanted to stay a little longer, but the monkey wouldn't have it.

* * *

P.I.G. was ecstatic about the impending drama. Once again, both Tiffany and Marcus had called minutes apart, saying they were on the way. Just to put more shit in the mix, he called Red's son to claim the bounty. He sat back smugly and awaited the fireworks.

And fireworks were exactly what Marcus had in store for P.I.G. He parked in front and tucked the forty-caliber pistol in his pants. He had fucked up all the dope money from robbing Pony and turned exclusively to robbery. In his previous armed robberies, Marcus committed two murders. He heard about the price on his head and knew his days were numbered. The realization that his time on Earth had run its course only fueled his mayhem. He brazenly refused to wear a mask, not caring who recognized him. Besides Red's sons, half of Atlanta was gunning for him.

Earl opened the door for Marcus and stepped aside as he'd done a hundred times before. "What up?" he said, not caring for a reply.

Marcus didn't give him one. Instead, he whipped out his pistol and shot Earl in the leg. He almost liked Earl, and that prevented him from aiming at his head.

Earl went down hard, screaming in pain as the other occupants screamed in fear.

"You!" Marcus yelled, pointing the weapon at Blast. "Bring me the money and the dope."

Instead of complying, Blast ignored him and ran to tend to Earl. Despite the intense fear, P.I.G. caught the affection his wife showed Earl.

"Get up, you fat bastard," Marcus said, turning his attention to P.I.G.

P.I.G. was frozen with fear, unable to move until the pistol collided with his forehead. He jumped from his chair and waddled down the hall with Marcus in tow.

The crackheads saw the opportunity to flee and took it. The frightened crowd passed Tiffany on the walk as they fled.

Tiffany's instinct to flee the obvious danger was betrayed by her thirst for drugs. Common sense told her to run, but the gorilla told her to stay, leaving her stuck in her place.

Before she could decide which way to move, Marcus came running out, bags in hand. When they came face to face, a scowl spread across his face as he raised the pistol to hers.

Tiffany felt no fear. Instead, a smile spread across her face. *No more pain,* she thought and closed her eyes. She felt no pain when the shot rang out. The next shot caused her to open her eyes, and she could see that the bullets were coming from two of Red's sons, who had just pulled up.

Instead of running away, Marcus pulled a second forty-caliber and ran toward them, with both guns blazing. He caught a round to his torso that didn't even slow him down. By the time he reached the curb, his guns were empty and his attackers deceased.

Two police officers who were patting down a shoplifter across the street watched the entire gunfight in shock. They abandoned the petty collar and rushed to join the fray.

Marcus pointed his guns at the approaching officers, who instinctively ducked for cover. Marcus repeatedly pulled the triggers of the empty weapons.

When the officers realized that he was out of ammo, they moved in. The young white cop, looking for his first kill, raised his gun to fire. He had been anticipating killing a suspect since the academy, and now he had the chance. If his partner had not hit him first with a TASER, Marcus would have been dead. The 50,000 volts of electricity dropped him to the pavement, shaking and slobbering.

Miraculously, Tiffany, who hadn't budged during the entire shootout, was unharmed. When the shooting stopped, she came out of her trance and made a move toward her car.

The first of what would eventually be dozens of police cars pulled up, blocking her car. She aborted that plan and walked up the street. A bus pulled to a stop, and Tiffany quickly fell in line to board it. When she settled back into her seat, she realized she was headed in the direction of her parents' house. Tiffany was headed home.

* * *

"Oh my God! Thank you, Jesus!" Mrs. Williams screamed at the sight of her daughter standing at the door. She squeezed Tiffany so tightly that all the air rushed from her lungs. "Let me see you!" she said, pulling away to inspect her child. The drastic changes she saw brought tears to her eyes. Tiffany had lost a great deal of weight and looked ashen. However, she could not see the majority of the damage because it was internal. "Don't you worry 'bout a thing," Mrs. Williams said, embracing her child again. "Mama got you now."

The show of affection caused Tiffany to begin crying as well. The two women stood there at the front door, hugging and crying, until Mrs. Williams pulled her inside.

"First, let me fix you something to eat," Tiffany's mother said, dragging her toward the kitchen. "Me and your daddy gon' help you. Everything gon' be all right," her mother rattled on. She was pulling out half of the refrigerator to heat up for her child as she spoke.

"Noooo!" Tiffany screamed, startling her busy mother.

"What? What's wrong, baby?" her mother asked, unaware that she was talking to Tiffany's demons and not Tiffany herself.

"Huh? Oh, nothing, Mama. I'm sorry," Tiffany said, embarrassed by the outburst.

"Do it! Take it!" the demon demanded as the monkey on her back began squealing in her ears. The combination of the two destructive forces caused Tiffany to close her eyes in a futile attempt to block them out.

"Oh, where is my phone? Let me call your daddy," Tiffany's mother said, looking around. "I'll be right back, baby," she said, remembering that she had left it on her dresser. She rushed off to retrieve it.

"That's right," the demon said, comforting Tiffany as she lifted her mother's purse from the kitchen counter. She grabbed the wallet and key before slipping into the garage as her mother descended the stairs.

"Baby?" Mrs. Williams called out curiously, looking around the empty kitchen. Her eyes focused on her open purse when she heard the garage door begin to open and her car start.

"Tiffany!" she asked, opening the door to the garage. Mrs. Williams grabbed the door handle of the car and made eye contact with her daughter. She realized she was looking into the eyes of a stranger. She was slow releasing the handle and got dragged out of the garage. Mrs. Williams lost her grip and tumbled down the driveway as her daughter sped off in her car.

CHAPTER 27

Marcus spent over a month in Grady Hospital recuperating from the gunshot wound that had almost killed him. To his dismay, he pulled through. His only consolation was that the state was seeking the death penalty. He was tired of his life and ready to go. Neighboring Dekalb County had linked his guns to two murders and was in line to prosecute him as well.

It was pure coincidence that his first court date fell on the same day in front of the same judge as P.I.G.'s, who had been arrested and charged with the drugs found in his yard. P.I.G.'s lawyers assured him that the charges would be dropped. After all, the drugs and money were found outside, on Marcus. They knew he'd robbed P.I.G., but they also knew no one could prove it. Of course, P.I.G. wasn't gonna tell them he'd gotten robbed for the four kilos.

Marcus's mother, along with his sister and her kids, unknowingly sat right behind P.I.G. and Blast in the courtroom. The time in the hospital and off the street had been kind to Marcus. He had put on some weight and got his color back.

His court-appointed lawyer begged him to cop out and

avoid a death penalty. The public defender fully intended to sell him out, but he didn't want his death on his conscience.

Marcus initially refused, preferring death to life imprisonment. It took his mother's tearful appeals to finally agree to take a deal. Marcus accepted life without parole on the two murders and planned to do the same in the next county as well.

When P.I.G. saw Marcus in the courtroom, he openly glared at him. He felt a sense of security since the man was cuffed and flanked by two deputies. Still, Marcus was pissed when their eyes met. "Oh, you hard now?" Marcus demanded with a demented chuckle. "I shoulda kilt yo' fat ass!"

P.I.G. shuddered in fear and unconsciously reached up and felt the scar left by Marcus's gun. He was embarrassed at the memory of his bladder releasing when Marcus put the gun in his mouth. He could still taste metal and hear the sound of the barrel clicking against his teeth.

To P.I.G.'s relief, the outburst caused the deputies to quickly remove Marcus from the courtroom. When his mother began wailing, she was also removed, followed by his sister and her kids. After the murder of a judge and a court reporter in the same room a few years back, there was zero tolerance.

When P.I.G.'s case was called, one of the high-priced lawyers got up and did his song and dance. At the end of the spiel, the judge had to agree that there wasn't enough evidence to go forward. He then admonished the overzealous prosecutor about bringing undeveloped cases in front of him, wasting the city's time and money.

The police department was embarrassed about P.I.G. getting off and resorted to harassment. P.I.G.'s main house was thirty-eight hot. They would post up in front of his house in an effort to shut him down.

Since P.I.G.'s other traphouses did the majority of his business, the boycott was in vain. His main house still served to entertain him, so he kept a small amount of drugs on hand to sustain Blast and his jesters. He had moved Earl to run out of the traphouses in an attempt to keep him and Blast apart. He didn't miss the affection she showed him during the robbery, and he made her pay for it every day.

Every night, P.I.G. staged drug-fueled orgies to add to his porno collection. By far, his favorite footage was Tiffany's masturbation scene. He played it daily, forcing Blast to blow him while he watched.

* * *

Tiffany was too hot for the clubs with deputies in search of her. She tricked exclusively with older white men. They came quick and paid well, although some had rather weird fetishes. For an additional fee, she would spank or even piss on a john. For a slightly higher fee, the john could spank or piss on her.

She was still driving her mother's Cadillac until one night a bored patrol officer decided to run all the plates at the hotel. When the car came back as stolen, a wrecker was called to tow it away. Tiffany sneaked out the back window of her room just before the police came knocking.

Scoring good coke was an everyday challenge. The few penitentiary-bound renegades who were foolish enough to play the motels strictly sold bullshit. Tiffany was forced to smoke whipped cocaine for days before running down some glass.

After the shootout at P.I.G.'s, she was too afraid to return, especially since her car was towed away, full of drug para-phernalia—not to mention she had witnessed men die. It was just more baggage for her heavily burdened soul to carry.

A chance meeting with a former acquaintance would change her fate.

"Hey, um…" Tiffany said, desperately trying to recall the name belonging to the familiar face.

"Rico," the man replied with a furrowed brow as he recognized what was left of Tiffany. He was a regular at Club Chocolate and remembered when she first started working at the door. He remembered how, a few months later, Mike charged him $1,500 to trick with her.

Tiffany remembered he had good coke, and she wanted some. Since she had already tricked with him before and she knew he enjoyed it and paid well, she decided to offer him herself and save her money for later. "You still be holding?" Tiffany asked seductively.

"No doubt," Rico responded, feeling himself stiffen at the memory of their hour together. "What you tryina do?"

"Shit. Come on and get your dick sucked," Tiffany said cheerfully.

Rico broke her off a few grams after she did the deed, then gave her his number. "Say, shawty, my people having a bachelor party tonight. You should come through and dance," he said as Tiffany exited his car.

"I don't know," Tiffany replied, leery of doing private parties. She preferred to stick to her white client base, even though it was dwindling, along with her weight.

"Come on, lil mama. It's only a couple guys, and they all ballers," Rico urged.

"Just dance?" Tiffany asked dubiously.

"Yeah, just dance…and you ain't gon' be the only girl,"

Rico added.

When Tiffany finally acquiesced, Rico gave her the name of the motel and some money for a cab.

Tiffany rushed off to smoke the first decent blow she'd had in weeks. As soon as she exhaled her first pull, she called the number Rico had given her. "I'm there!" she said excitedly.

When Rico finished that call, he quickly made another. "What up, shawty?" he said when the call was answered. "Man, I got us a sho nuff freak for the night. Bitch must be part anaconda, straight eat a dick," he said animatedly. With that call, a gangbang was set in motion, as call after call was made.

* * *

Tiffany knew she was in trouble as soon as she walked into the hotel room. There were twenty young, rowdy black men, all drinking and smoking heavily. All her instincts told her to leave, but she stayed anyway. "I thought you said it was only a few people?" she whispered through clenched teeth as Rico let her in. "And where are the other girls?" she asked when she noticed she was the only female in the room.

"They coming, so you may as well get some money before they do," Rico reasoned.

Tiffany knew having the lone pussy in a room full of dudes wasn't a good look, but the lure of easy money and good coke propelled her. After dancing a couple of songs in a thong set, Tiffany was handed a drink. Parched from her movements, she downed it without hesitation.

Rico smiled knowingly as he watched her swallow the drink in a couple of gulps.

Tiffany couldn't taste the date rape drug that laced her

drink but felt its effects midway through the next song. Time and space slowed to a crawl as the chemicals invaded her senses. By the end of the song, she was dead on her feet. The powerful drug incapacitated her movements, but she could see and hear everything around her. So, when the plan to run a train on her was announced, there was nothing she could do or say.

She could hear them arguing about who was first as they laid her out on the floor. Her skimpy underwear was peeled off, and Rico climbed inside of her. Tiffany tried to scream, but nothing came out. Instead, her open mouth was taken as an invitation and quickly filled. She watched helplessly as the two men pounded away, grinning wildly. When they finished, they were replaced by two more, followed by two more.

Over the next few hours, Tiffany was repeatedly raped by the men. Some took her over and over, taking smoke breaks in between. She was ravaged vaginally, orally, and anally. The laughter of her attackers rang in her ears hours after they left her alone on the hotel room floor.

* * *

The next morning, when the hotel maid entered the room, she thought she had come across a dead body. The terrified Hispanic woman ran screaming from the room.

When EMS workers arrived, they found Tiffany covered in semen, urine, and filth from her bowels' release, but she was alive.

When she finally came around, she found herself hand-cuffed to a hospital bed at Grady Memorial. It took her a few minutes to get her bearings before the events surrounding her being in a hospital overwhelmed her. She closed her eyes tightly, attempting to flee from the memories with sleep. "Thank God it's over," Tiffany said, embracing the much-needed rest. She knew full well she would not be on the streets for some time to come. "It's finally over. Thank you, God," she rejoiced loudly before drifting off.

"Amen," her mother said quietly, unseen on the other side of the room.

* * *

A week and a hundred tests later, Tiffany was released to the sheriff's deputies and taken to the jail to await trial on felony theft charges.

A sympathetic judge accepted her lawyer's and the DA recommendations that she be treated as a first-time offender. She would have to complete a twelve-month lockdown rehabilitation program, followed by twelve months of probation. If she did, she would have a clean slate.

Her supportive parents agreed to make restitution to her employer and drop the charges for stealing the car.

The judge admonished her sternly and warned that this was her second chance and that she would not get a third. "Consider yourself lucky," he barked gruffly before bringing his gavel down.

Tiffany knew she was lucky at the very least. Even after all her time on the street, she was still disease and pregnancy free. Luck didn't seem to quite sum it up for her now. She was sure there had to be more to it than mere chance...divine intervention.

* * *

Wanda wasn't quite as lucky. Life on the streets, combined with a serious drug habit and full-blown AIDS, was taking its toll on the woman. Her body was so deteriorated that even the horniest of tricks turned their noses up at her and drove by. Only the most desperate or cheapest johns picked her up. They ended up paying twice for a romp with Wanda: once in cash and later with their health.

"You sure, boss?" P.I.G.'s new doorman asked curiously when he as ordered to let the sorry sight in.

"Hey, Wanda. How's my girl today?" P.I.G. said warmly as she entered. The hospitable greeting would be the only humanity she had coming. It was, in fact, a prelude to whatever licentious act P.I.G. could come up with.

Wanda had lost all shame many years earlier, yet humbling herself to P.I.G. still ate at her. She loathed the man to the core of her soul, but with no money or other options, she subjected herself to his whims.

The junkies in the room had only recently put their clothes back on from performing a particularly odious scene. At P.I.G.'s direction, the men had sex with the men and the girls with the girls. To add insult, he now replayed the footage while they smoked their recompense. As a result, they were feeling dejected and didn't care to freak with Wanda.

"I guess you'll just have to sweep up," P.I.G. said with a chuckle. This would be his crowning moment.

"Uh-uh! Don't do her like that!" Blast pleaded.

"Don't do her like what?" P.I.G. snapped. "She ain't gotta do nothing she don't wanna do."

"Ima do it," Wanda said meekly. She had accepted defeat, and P.I.G. was the winner.

Everyone in the room looked at each other curiously, wondering what the big deal about sweeping up could be. They were all too new to have witnessed the degrading act before.

Wanda knew what she was in for. She made her way over to P.I.G. and let the filthy Coogi dress fall to the floor. When she turned around and bent over, Blast gathered up her pipe and rocks and left the room. Wanda winced with pain when P.I.G. shoved the toy broom in her rectum.

"Get busy," P.I.G. demanded, setting her in motion.

Wanda squatted and swayed her hips to work the broom. She began to sweep up.

Although no one found it the least bit amusing, they roared with laughter when P.I.G. did. They knew to laugh on command when P.I.G. said something was funny, whether it was entertaining or not. Their highs and their lives depended on it.

"You missed a spot!" P.I.G. said with a laugh, and the crowd joined him.

Tears fell freely from Wanda's eyes as she swept the room, in total pain and embarrassment.

After what seemed like an eternity, P.I.G. allowed her to stop. "Blast!" P.I.G. yelled as he stopped the camera. "Get yo' ass out here."

Blast came out and glared dangerously at her husband as Wanda pulled the broom out of her ass and slid her dress on.

"Give this lil bitch something for cleaning up," P.I.G. said with a chuckle, eliciting more forced laughter from the spectators.

"Ain't nothing left," Blast announced firmly. "I told you to send for Earl." The only drugs left were hers, and she wasn't about to part with them for his bullshit. He ran through several ounces a day with his freaks, and she'd be damned if she gave up hers.

"Oh well." P.I.G. shrugged nonchalantly. "I guess you'll have to come back tomorrow. I'll let ya sweep up again."

The smokers all chuckled at the dis, glad it wasn't directed at them.

That was the proverbial straw that broke the camel's back. Something snapped inside of Wanda as a lifetime of disappointment and bad memories flooded her brain.

As she reached in her purse, she could see her stepdad sneaking into her room at night, followed by her stepbrother. She recalled every lie told to her by Mike and others like him, the pathetic lies that turned her into a prostitute and a stripper, only to be chumped off for Tiffany. She remembered every trick and every dick.

The room fell silent as Wanda produced the little raggedy gun from her purse. Her hand shook wildly as she pointed the weapon at P.I.G.'s wide face. Wanda's hand was shaking so hard that the clip fell out of the gun, causing the room to erupt in laughter.

The doorman, who had been easing up to disarm Wanda, fell back and joined the revelry.

Then an explosion from the small gun reverberated in the suddenly silent room. Everyone looked around at each other in shock.

P.I.G. had a confused look on his face, as if trying to figure out what had just happened. The small-caliber projectile had entered his nostril so cleanly it took a few seconds before he or anyone else knew he was hit. By the time he realized what happened, he was dead. His huge head slumped forward, causing blood to pour from his nose.

The junkies, along with the doorman, all ran out of the

house.

Wanda smiled at the sight of her dead tormenter, then turned on her heels and left as well.

Blast simply walked to the back and continued smoking. When the police arrived an hour later, that was where they found her…still smoking. She was arrested for possession, but luckily, the police response time was so slow that she'd smoked her stash down to an ounce, thus avoiding a trafficking charge. That meant the difference between rehab versus twenty years.

Once she arrived at the jail, she used her one call to contact Earl. "It's over, baby. The pig is dead," she said, relieved. After explaining what happened, she told him to collect the money from the houses and shut everything down. She gave him her bond information and waited for him to come and get her.

Instead, Earl gathered up almost $300,000 from the houses and took flight—took *a* flight, to be exact. He paid cash for a one-way ticket to his birthplace on the small Caribbean island of Tobago, all courtesy of his former employers.

CHAPTER 28

As fate would have it, Blast and Tiffany ended up in the same rehabilitation center. The two women were cordial to each other when they met, but they generally tried to avoid each other. They shared a legacy of pain and degradation that they didn't care to be reminded of. They wanted the past to stay where it belonged: in the past.

This came easier for Tiffany, who had mended her relationship with her parents. They were at the center every weekend for visitation. Their unwavering support and forgiveness was essential to Tiffany's rehabilitation.

* * *

Blast, on the other hand, was all alone. When Earl ran off, she had no one to turn to. She had not spoken with her family in Mississippi in so long that she didn't even know them anymore. She had millions of dollars but not one friend. She had trusted Earl, and that didn't turn out well at all. She had plenty of money to replace the $300,000 he absconded with, but no amount of money could fix her broken heart.

* * *

Tiffany's parents had told her they would not be coming to visit one weekend, so she was surprised to hear her name called over the loudspeaker for visitation. "Okaaay! I wonder who this could be," Tiffany sang giddily as she dressed for her visit. Since there were no classes, group sessions, or mail on the weekends, they were dreadfully slow. Spending a couple of hours with loved ones was always a welcomed reprieve.

"Table Five," the guard supervising the visitation area directed as Tiffany entered.

She stared at the familiar face, blinking to be sure her eyes weren't playing tricks on her. Every time she opened her eyes, she expected him to be gone, but there he was. "Oh my God! Is that you!?" she asked, embracing the man. "What's that on your face…and on your head?" Tiffany asked when they separated from their hug.

"This is a beard, and this is a Kufi," Carlos said, matter-of-factly.

"So you're one of them Moslems now?" Tiffany asked as they took their seats.

"It's Muslim, and yes. *Ash hadoo anla illaha illallah!*" he replied cheerfully.

"I have no idea what that means. It's pretty though." Tiffany laughed.

"I said, 'There is no God but the one God, and Muhammad, peace be upon him, is His messenger'," Carlos replied seriously. "Oh, and it's Ali now."

"So your girl a Muslim too?" Tiffany asked, turning up her lips.

"I'm not with her anymore. I'm taking some time to get myself in order before I find a wife," he replied.

"I can relate," Tiffany said, waving her hand around the room. "Tryina get right too."

For the next few hours, the couple talked about everything under the sun. This was the most conversation they'd had in years. Tiffany had a million questions about religion, and Carlos answered them all as best he could.

When the guards announced that their time was up, Tiffany made Carlos promise to return the following week. He also gave her a small Qur'an that he kept with him.

During the week, Carlos and Tiffany enjoyed marathon phone conversations as they rebuilt their friendship. Tiffany was so enthralled with her Qur'an that they spent hours discussing it.

Tiffany's parents were dismayed when she asked them not to come up for visitation, but they were fine with it when she told them Carlos was coming . They were very fond of him and knew he was a good young man.

"What's wrong?" Carlos asked urgently when he saw Tiffany's tears at their next visit.

"You think God—or Allah—can forgive me?" she asked, sobbing.

Carlos lifted her head with his hand to make eye contact before they spoke. "When you accept Islam, all your past sins are forgiven," he assured her.

"Okay. So what I gotta do?" Tiffany asked eagerly.

"What do you mean?" Carlos asked, unsure of the question.

"To be a Muslim, to be forgiven, what I gotta do?" she replied.

"Just repeat after me...*Ash-hadoo anla illah illallah, wa ash haddo anna Muhammadan rasoulullah,*" he said.

When she was unable to repeat it verbatim, he broke it

down into segments, and she got it.

"Now you gotta turn a back flip, and you in," Carlos said seriously.

"You for real?" Tiffany asked, incredulous. "I can't turn no flip!"

"Just kidding, Fatima," Carlos laughed.

"What you call me?" Tiffany demanded with a frown.

"Fatima," Carlos said seriously. "That's the name of the prophet's—peace be upon him—daughter, Ali's wife."

"Oh," Tiffany said, calming down from thinking he'd called her some other girl's name. "Oh!" she exclaimed excitedly when she finally caught on. "So are you asking me…!" Tiffany yelled, unable to even get it out.

"Yes, sister, I'm asking you to marry me," Carlos said sincerely.

"Yes, of course! Of course!" Tiffany said, still screaming. "I mean, *insha-Allah*!" She chuckled, embarrassed by her outburst.

* * *

Over the next eight months, Carlos and Tiffany grew closer. Besides his weekly visits, they spent hours on the phone.

Tiffany embraced her new way of life with zeal. She read everything she could get her hands on and ordered more books when she finished those. Carlos was both amazed and pleased at how much she learned; she was even teaching him things he didn't know.

When the program ran its course, the residents were free to go. They had a van to take people with no rides to the train station. Since the majority of them had long since burned their bridges, most took the van.

In the end, only Tiffany and Blast remained. They were both hoping their rides showed up quickly to avoid conversation. Tiffany knew Carlos and her parents were en route, but Blast was looking for Earl. Even though she had not heard one word from him or even knew his whereabouts, she kept up hope. She knew what they shared was true love, and she held faith in that.

When Carlos's truck pulled up, Tiffany ran down to meet it. Halfway down the steps, she stopped and went back. She gave Blast a hug that spoke volumes without uttering one word.

"Go. I'm all right," Blast said, fighting the urge to cry.

"You sure? We can give you a ride," Tiffany offered as they broke their embrace.

"No. Earl is coming. He's just running late," Blast said, believing it herself.

"Okay," Tiffany said sadly. She knew no one was coming for Blast, even if Blast wouldn't admit it. "Take care," she said over her shoulder as she went to the truck.

* * *

After a tearful reunion with her family, Carlos steered the truck toward Atlanta.

"Where we going?" Tiffany asked curiously as they passed the exit that would have taken them home.

"To the masjid on Fourteenth Street…to get married," Carlos said proudly.

"You asking or telling?" Tiffany shot back playfully.

"Telling!" her mother and father replied in unison from the backseat.

"Okay! Dang! Let's go get married then." Tiffany laughed.

After a short Islamic service, Carlos and Tiffany dropped her parents off at their house before heading to their own. Carlos had purchased a new home in a surrounding county several months earlier, but he'd waited for Tiffany's release so they could move into it together.

* * *

Blast finally admitted to herself that no one was coming. She called a taxi to take her to her house. "Girl, you healthy and rich," she told herself to combat the urge to cry. Still, she gave the driver the directions to the house that Earl had run for P.I.G. before he left.

She accepted the fact that Earl was gone, but she still hoped he wasn't. Besides, there was no way she was going to step foot in the house of horror on Moreland Avenue ever again. She debated whether she should sell it or burn it to the ground.

Blast thanked the driver twice, once verbally and then again by allowing him to keep the change. She fished out the keys and entered the musty house. Her heart sank again when she saw it was indeed uninhabited.

"Oh well." She shrugged. "Five hours, three cars, and two mill," she said, counting her blessings. She then set about opening windows to air the dank house.

Blast got misty-eyed when she got to the master bedroom, the place she and Earl stole moments together when they could. An envelope taped to the mirror instantly caught her attention. She smiled at the familiar handwriting as she tore into the package. Blast disregarded what she thought were brochures that fell out, eager to get a letter. To her surprise, it wasn't dated a year earlier, but only the day before. She fumbled to get it open and read it as quick as she could:

"Hey, baby. Wipe that smile off your face! I'm sorry I left the way I did, but it was for the best. Had I bailed you out that night, we would have both went back to the same life. We would have ended up in jail, dead, or worse...still junkies. I'm clean now. Have been since the day I left. I'm at home now—our home—waiting on you. Enclosed is a one-way ticket. I'll see you tonight. Love, Earl."

"I'm coming, baby!" Blast screamed, scrambling to pick up the fallen tickets.

CHAPTER 29

After pleading out to two life sentences in Atlanta, Marcus took his other murder charges to trial just for the hell of it. Dekalb County gave him two more life sentences without the possibility of parole.

At the age of twenty-one, he was facing living the next forty or fifty years in prison , until he died. They were never gonna let him out. He spent six months at a diagnostic prison undergoing a battery of physical and mental evaluations. Then he was sent to a Level Five prison to serve his time.

New arrivals came into the prison system every Tuesday and Thursday. This allowed the predators to develop a routine. When the new inmates were brought into the dorm, the robbing crew would duck off into a cell and see who was who.

If someone was a known snitch, they wouldn't be allowed to stay. If they were bait, they were robbed. If they got robbed and didn't get anyone back, they were getting fucked next. The Georgia prison system's motto was "Fuck, fight, or wash clothes." If you were fucking, then so be it. If you fought, you earned respect. If you opted to wash clothes, it was only a matter of time before you were fucking.

Marcus was spotted the moment he walked into the cell house. "I know dat ain't the nigga dat kilt my daddy," Red's son, Lil Red, announced. He was serving a life sentence of his own for armed robbery and murder.

"Who?" his homeboy, Willie B, asked, crowding the small window in the door. Willie B earned his nickname by looking just like the legendary gorilla from the Atlanta Zoo, and just like his namesake, he was a gorilla.

Lil Red was about to rush out and attack until Willie B restrained him.

"Chill, shawty. Let's wait till after count," he reasoned.

"That's what's up," Lil Red agreed.

The prison took a headcount every four hours. That was the only time the correction officers ever came in. The inmates had from count to count to do whatever they wanted to do.

"Yeah, Ima fuck dat lil nigga real good," Willie B announced eagerly. He had been locked up since age ten and had never been with a woman, yet even though the only pussy he ever had was boy pussy, he didn't think of himself as gay.

Lil Red hated the homosexual culture of the prison system, but he intended to let Willie B rape Marcus as part of the torture. They would have four hours with him, and he didn't plan to kill Marcus until the last moment. They recruited another one of their homeboys to take part in the murder.

When the time came, Marcus's cellmate was lured out before the trio rushed in. Marcus was busy arranging his locker box when he was attacked.

As Lil Red and Shakey pummeled Marcus, Willie B undressed. "Strip dat ho," Willie B ordered, stroking his erection with vigilance.

Marcus soon found himself tied, face down, on the bunk. He screamed in vain through the gag as Willie B climbed on top of him. Marcus's screams became shrill as Willie B pushed inside of him.

Lil Red turned away, disgusted, as Shakey watched curiously.

"Kill me! Jus' kill me!" Marcus begged.

Meanwhile, Willie B was having the time of his life. He wished he was alone with his prey and wished he had more time with him. He wanted to make love to Marcus, to flip him over and fuck him face to face and kiss him in the mouth.

A strange thing happened as Marcus was being raped. He finally managed to work the gag free from his mouth, but instead of screaming, he laughed.

"That fuck nigga like dat shit!" Lil Red yelled, enraged that the dude they were supposed to be torturing and killing was having fun. "I'm finna murk dis nigga," he said, stepping forward.

Marcus had been diagnosed as HIV positive, and he loved the fact that he was at least going to be taking one of them with him.

Willie B knew his time was up and finished up with a quick thrust. He rolled of just as Lil Red and Shakey began beating Marcus with the padlocks tied to their belts.

After bludgeoning Marcus to death, they slid his body under the bed, where it wouldn't be seen until the next count came up short two hours later. Willie B missed his new lover already and thought about him as he sucked on a cigarette.

On four life sentences, Marcus served just under four months, and finally, he was a free man.

EPILOGUE

"**Y**es, dear?" Fatima sang to her husband as they drove along the interstate.

"Yes what?" Ali asked, puzzled by the statement. "I ain't call you."

"I coulda sworn...never mind," she replied, feeling a little silly. She was sure she had heard her name called.

"Tiffany!" the voice called again, louder this time.

"No! Leave me alone!" Tiffany screamed as she realized who was calling her.

"What's wrong? Is it the baby?" Carlos asked, rubbing his free hand on her protruding belly.

"Huh? Oh, nothing," Tiffany stammered, embarrassed by the outburst. She smiled and placed her hand on top of his as their son kicked inside of her.

"You can't ignore me forever," the demon said with a chuckle. *"I'll be waiting..."*

the end

G STREET CHRONICLES

 PRESENTS

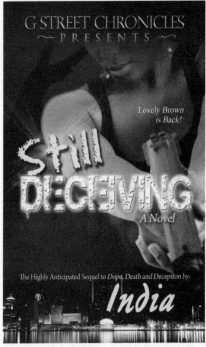

Lovely Brown was living the good life as Detroit's top drug dealer, operating under the alias LB. Everything was going smooth until her father Lucifer escaped from prison, ready to return to the throne and destroy anyone in his path, including Lovely. While running for her life, she was also being investigated by the Feds and simultaneously set-up for the murder of her mafia connects' nephew. This resulted in a ONE MILLION DOLLAR bounty being placed on her head. Achieving the impossible, Lovely managed to escape unscathed.

Now, five years after she left all the Dope, Death and Deception behind and she's finally living a normal life, things get complicated. Issues from her past come right to her front door. Once again Lovely finds herself in a bad situation with her back against the wall—looking sideways at everyone in her corner. Lies have been told and love has been tested.

Just when she thought things were over, it looks as if someone is Still Deceiving!

www.gstreetchronicles.com

Be sure to check out India's series.
It began here . . .

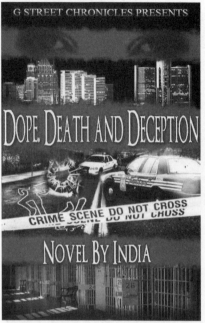

Meet Lovely Brown, a 20 year old from Detroit, MI that has witnessed too much! After her father was sentenced to major time behind bars her mother turns to drugs and is later found dead because of it. She is left to take care of her younger sister after her older sister bails! She s been homeless and hungry, taking various street jobs to put food on the table for her baby sister Tori, but after a case of mistaken identity Lovely is left all alone with no family because they ve all become victims of the streets, in one way or another. She vows to take vengeance into her own hands and shut down the dope game by becoming one of it s major players, operating under the name LB. Everything was running smoothly until she finds out that she has a 1 MILLION dollar bounty placed on her head and seemingly overnight everything begins to fall apart. In the mist of her chaos she falls in love with a guy that she knows little about. They have both been keeping secrets but his could prove to be deadly for her! Immediately she thinks of an exit strategy but will she make it out the game alive?

Mz. Robinson

5 STAR REVIEWS!!!

WELCOME TO THE JUNGLE!!

The King, raised in the hood with his family, saw a lot of suffering. He witnessed death and destruction within his own family—poverty and desperation of his own people. Instead of being part of the problem, he became part of the solution and rose to the top of his game. In his mind…it was survival.

After an encounter with a brilliant scientist, King began to plot something so huge, that no one would see it coming or be able to stop the cycle…not even the police.

5 STAR REVIEWS!!!

Lies, deceit and murder ran rampant throughout the city of Atlanta. Real and his lady, Constance, were living in the lap of luxury, with fancy cars, expensive clothes and a million dollar home until someone close to them alerted the feds to their illegal activity.

At the blink of an eye their perfect life was turned upside down. Just as Real was sorting things out on the home front, the head of Miami's most powerful Cartel gave him an ultimatum that would eventually force him back into the life he had swore off forever. Knowing this lifestyle would surely put Constance in danger, he made plans to send her away until the score was settled but things spiraled out of control. Now Real and Constance are in a fight for survival where friends become enemies and murder is essential. Atlanta's underworld to Miami's most affluent community—no stone was left unturned as Real fought to keep Constance safe while attempting to regain control of the lifestyle he once would kill for.

From the city of Atlanta to the cell block of Georgia's most dangerous prison, life under the City Lights would never be the same.

www.gstreetchronicles.com

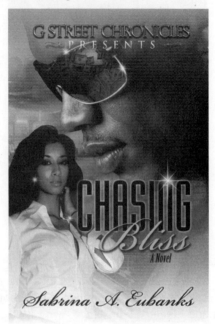

Name: _____

Address: _____

City/State: _____

Zip: _____

ALL BOOKS ARE $10 EACH

QTY	TITLE	PRICE
	Trap House	
	Still Deceiving	
	City Lights	
	A-Town Veteran	
	Beastmode	
	Executive Mistress	
	Essence of a Bad Girl	
	Dope, Death and Deception	
	Dealt the Wrong Hand	
	Married to His Lies	
	What We Won't Do for Love	
	Two Face	
	Family Ties	
	Blocked In	
	Drama	
	Shipping & Handling ($4 per book)	

TOTAL $ _____

To order online visit

www.gstreetchronicles.com

Send cashiers check or money order to:

G Street Chronicles

P.O. Box 490082   College Park, GA 30349